Fate Intertwined

Book One

of

Intertwined Series

Delia Duke

Love is when he gives you a

piece of your soul that you

never knew was missing.

-Torquato Tasso

Content Warning

This story contains explicit sexual content, profanity, and topics that may be sensitive to some readers.

Chapter 1

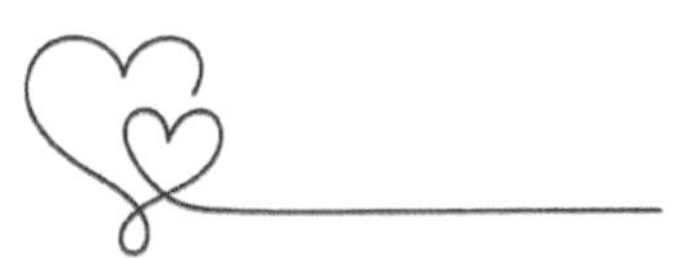

With peppy, enthusiastic steps, I walked through the terminal of LaGuardia Airport and headed for the exit. Hipsters around me seemed just as excited to be there. This was my hometown, New York City, the largest city in the world, which I had left a long time ago. The reason behind that decision was something I tried not to delve into. Neither did I want to think about the life I had lived.

As I dragged my carry-on through the vast terminal, strangers bumped against my suitcase. Clumsy little kids blundered into it and then waddled onward. Huge backpacks weighed them down, but their excitement to explore my city could be heard in their laughter.

The summer airport crowd was insane as usual, but it wasn't like the season made any difference. New York City airports were perpetually crowded, swarming with people no matter what year or day.

Behind me, an impatient man was trying to outsmart everyone and find some way to get ahead of the crowd. I turned around and smiled. The man's irritation faded as he reciprocated.

See, Abby? I am taking your "a killer smile is the best weapon" mantra seriously.

My struggle with foot traffic ended when I exited the airport through the automatic double door, only to be greeted by a new challenge. Scorching heat enveloped me like a thick blanket, causing my cool linen sundress to cling to my skin. The torturous eighty-five-degree heat, with suffocating ninety percent humidity, wasn't much different from what I'd had to deal with in Boston. Both can be described in five exact words: excessively hot and oppressively muggy.

After growing up in New York and spending many years in Boston, I should've been used to this weather by now. I wasn't.

"Ivy!"

I turned around at the sound of a man calling my name.

"Well, well. Look who decided to show up this morning." His familiar voice pulled me out of my thoughts as I reached the pick-up area.

I ran up to Ryan, who greeted me with a bright smile and open arms. I matched his enthusiasm with a bone-crushing hug. Bone-crushing by my standards—like a gazelle crushing a cheetah.

"It took you only, what, eight years to come home, my sweet little sister?" Ryan said, as I held onto him tightly.

"You're making it sound like we haven't seen each other in all these years."

"Of course we have. But only when *I* visited *you*."

I ignored that part and finally let go of him, still smiling and unable to contain my excitement. Yes, it had taken me that long to come back, but I was here with him now. That was all that mattered. Wasn't it?

We walked to his car. I couldn't help but notice the three women that walked by and scanned Ryan from head to toe. One even bit her lip, liking what she saw. In his typical fashion, Ryan looked straight ahead, oblivious to the attention he was receiving.

I spelled it out for him. "Those women were checking you out, big brother."

"Well, the creep that just walked past us was checking *you* out, too." Displeased, he raised a judgmental eyebrow. "I guess I'm no longer the only McAlister turning heads in this town."

I glanced back, only to find a guy ogling at me. He wasn't alone, either. In fact, he was holding hands with a pretty brunette. *Creepy to walk with your girlfriend and stare at another woman.*

"He's cute. I like him."

Ryan's expression turned grave.

"Seriously? I can't call a guy cute now, even when I'm clearly joking?"

"You have beauty, brains, and money, Ivy. You should be very careful who you like."

That earned him a huge eye roll. My brother had absolutely no sense of humor. Ryan put my suitcase in the trunk of his Mercedes sedan while I walked to the passenger side and got in.

"How was your flight?" he asked, as he got behind the wheel. Apparently, he had decided to change his tone and start over as we pulled out of the curbside. "I can't tell you how happy I am to finally see you here. Your bag, though…"

"What about it?"

"It seems…light. Don't tell me that after being away all this time, you came for only a few days?"

"You ask a lot of questions. Should I turn around and go back?" My lip twitched, trying to hide my grin.

"I'm sorry. I didn't mean to upset you."

"You really can't tell when I'm joking, can you?" I was getting increasingly annoyed by his reaction. "Did you leave your sense of humor at home today?"

He narrowed his eyes, but instantly relaxed.

"Look, Ryan. I'm really sorry it took me so long to get home. I wanted to come back when I was ready, and now I am. I feel bad that you've had to put up with such a lousy sister."

"Don't be ridiculous. We're family. Actually, we're all that's *left* of the McAlister family. Like it or not, you're stuck with me forever."

I had put distance between us, even though I knew it would hurt him. But with me, my brother was still a softie. What I had done was a necessity. What I was going to do next was a compulsion.

I came back for him and to relive my old life, even if only for a few days.

Although Ryan was ten years older, and we didn't live in the same city or speak regularly, our sibling bond remained strong. I was thankful to our parents for breaking the cycle of having one child and choosing to have two instead. Now that they were gone, at least Ryan and I still had each other.

I decided to steer our discussion to lighter topics. "I came to spend time with you, Ryan. I'm here until next Saturday. Since we haven't spoken much in the last few months, I should probably fill you in on some stuff." I took a deep breath and jumped straight into the unpleasant discussion. "I enrolled in the business program we discussed a while back."

"So, you're staying at Harvard." He stated it less like a question and more like a fact he needed to say out loud to be able to believe.

A shadow of sadness settled over his face. Thankfully, he didn't push further. I wasn't expecting anything different, so I stayed quiet and let him digest the news.

"I'm glad you took some time off and came," he eventually said. "Even better that you came today."

"What's so special about today? Are you getting married over the weekend?" I teased. The Ryan I knew worked crazy hours and had no time for a girlfriend, let alone for getting married and building a life with someone.

"Smartass." He rolled his eyes, which he also got in return from me. "Today is the opening of our new Midtown hotel,

MoxTo. We're hosting an event there this evening, with some VIP clients and a few important guests. Would be nice if you could join, too, so people can stop speculating."

I raised an eyebrow and turned in my seat. "What are people saying?"

"That I have an imaginary sister. Or that she's tucked away somewhere in a high castle tower and I'm the monster brother who never lets her out in public." Ryan laughed at his own joke. Though he tried hard not to show it, I could tell that the assumptions upset him.

"People can be really melodramatic and nosy." I tried to lift his mood. "That being said, I would love to join you tonight. I have to go shopping for the perfect dress, though. After all, Ryan McAlister's sister has to make an entrance."

And, finally, there it was—that million-watt smile of his that I'd been waiting for. "Anything you want, Miss Ivy McAlister."

Honking cars, unruly traffic, a sea of people crossing the streets and milling around… New York City was a city that never slept. Manhattan, or "The City" as it was called by locals and visitors who knew the lingo, had been my home for fourteen years until it was time to go to high school.

I had so many wonderful memories tied to this city; but after we lost our parents nine years ago in a freak car accident, I sank deeper and deeper into the darkness. Terrible nightmares wouldn't let me sleep. Emptiness wouldn't let me live. I bounced between sad and angry and I couldn't find a way out of my misery.

Then, during that last summer at the McAlister family's vacation house in the Hamptons, everything changed. I distinctly remember that day because it changed my life completely.

I had told Ryan I didn't want to be around anyone. He either didn't hear me or chose to ignore me. I was in the pool when his best friends, Nick, Jonah, and Taber, came over. They had all met at Columbia University and had been inseparable since their freshman year of undergrad. After graduation, they took over their respective family businesses. With our parents no longer with us, Ryan had little choice but to do the same.

But at that time, my teenage hormones had kicked in. I developed a huge crush on Nick, the hottest of his friends, and I was crazy about his deep emerald-green eyes. My stomach flipped every time I saw him pulling into our driveway on his Ducati motorbike, a leather jacket accentuating his broad shoulders. I was pretty sure those reflective blue sunglasses became a fashion statement after he wore them. He was breathtaking in every sense of the word, and I was completely smitten by him.

Being a clueless teenager and not knowing how to act in front of a guy I liked, I decided that being rude and angry would be my best cover. Especially when Nick constantly referred to me as a kid, a teenager, a brat—anything to remind me he was out of my league and that my fantasies of him ever seeing me as something more than his best friend's little sister would never become reality.

Our ongoing quips were the start of our stupid and very one-sided relationship.

So, back to that particular hot summer day in the Hamptons: I was swimming laps when the boys showed up. I heard some banter and came out of the pool, only to find them fixing drinks and getting ready to jump in.

While passing me a towel, Nick's hand brushed over mine and a thousand volts of electricity ran from my head all the way to my toes. Our eyes met, and I saw it in his face, too—he was as shocked as I was.

Not knowing how to react, I instinctively stepped back and decided to hide my feelings behind my anger. I went over to Ryan and screamed at him for bringing his friends over.

I'll never forget the look of horror on Ryan's face. Shocked by my outburst, he, as usual, stayed calm. Unlike me, my big brother always keeps his feelings under control.

I walked away in a huff and hid in my bedroom with my nose in a book for the rest of the day.

Later that night, Ryan came over to talk to me. "What do you want to do with your life, Ivy?" he asked. "What would make you happy?"

I blurted out the first thing that came to my mind. "Move to Boston!"

"No. Not possible," he immediately said.

This led to another drawn-out argument, which only ended when I yelled, "Leave me alone!" and locked myself in my room.

I didn't leave for two whole days.

During that time, Ryan tried to reason with me. "Ivy, I'm sorry. Please. Just talk to me."

Still, I didn't open the door. Not because I was angry or perturbed, but because I was ashamed of myself for throwing a tantrum. I was a teenager, and I thought if I apologized, it would mean I was admitting my mistakes. Although I knew it was the right thing to do, I couldn't bring myself to actually do it.

My thoughts were beyond my control. Ryan was busy stepping into Dad's shoes and taking over the business. To demand more attention than I already needed seemed too selfish. I hid my nightmares as well as my sorrows because I didn't want to worry him, but they wouldn't let me make peace with the fact that Mom and Dad were gone.

The more I thought about moving to Boston, the more it made sense. A fresh start was what I needed. I was also desperate for the anonymity that Boston could provide. So, after two days of doing vigorous research, I joined the New England Academy in Beverly, Massachusetts, a suburb of Boston. It had a challenging curriculum to deal with my mental health. Also, if I wanted to get into Harvard, like I had told my parents ever since I was a little girl, I needed a place like that to get me to my goal.

Two days later, Nick's parents, Rosanne and Xavier, joined us at our Hamptons home. Without our parents, Ryan felt as lost as I was. He had no idea how to handle our new normal, much less how to handle a teenage sister. Rosanne and our mom had been best friends since their college days, so she took it upon herself to be there for us. Together with Xavier, they were the people Ryan could count on.

The next morning, when I joined them for breakfast, we discussed my reasons for wanting to move. I wasn't sure how I could tell them because I never told anyone about my nightmares; but in the end, I convinced them all.

Within a month, I was in Boston with a live-in nanny to watch over me—that was because I was still a minor. It was an arrangement I could live with, which was good, since there was no option for me to refuse.

I promised to spend every summer and every holiday in New York. And I did, at least for the holidays. At least at Rosanne and Xavier Branson's home in upstate New York. And at least while I was in high school.

After that, I found excuses. Internships, feeling under the weather, snowstorms preventing my plane from taking off, or not wanting to drive on icy roads. I had an unlimited list of ways to avoid them all.

In Boston, no one knew who I was. Whatever I achieved, it was because of my merit and not because of my name or the hefty sum of money in my bank accounts. No one associated Ivy McAlister with The McAlister Group. The idea that I was the second heir to the McAlister Real Estate fortune didn't cross anyone's mind. I lived my life the way I wanted to live it, because Boston gave me what I desperately needed.

A new beginning.

Nostalgia engulfed me as the elevator in our Upper West Side building took us to the penthouse. This building had been one of Dad's favorite purchases in the city. He'd loved it so much that he convinced mom to make it our home. I wasn't even born then, but that's what I heard growing up.

All the emotions that I had bottled up started coming in waves as the elevator ascended. *You aren't that person anymore. You don't cry. You don't let sadness swallow you, Ivy. This is the new you. Remember that.*

From the elevator to the mahogany double door, we walked along the stretch of the long corridor. Nothing had changed. Polished marble floor gleaming under the crystal chandeliers. Intricate details of gold-leaf moldings creating a sense of grandeur. When Ryan opened the door for me and invited me in, I held my breath.

And then my mouth practically fell open. "Whoa! What happened here?"

Furniture had been replaced, wallpaper removed, and fixtures changed. The only way I could have described my parents' home was "eclectic meets bohemia," instead of timeless sophistication and plush elegance. Suddenly, it didn't feel like I had come back to my parents' house at all.

Hold on, Ivy. Why did you want to return to the same place you ran away from? If you couldn't take all the sadness the house brought you, why expect Ryan to keep living with it for so many years?

"I'm sorry. I probably should've warned you about the changes," Ryan stated.

"You don't have to explain anything to me, Ryan. This is your house and you have every right to make any changes you want. You don't owe me an explanation." I turned to him and gave him a hug. "You and me, together. That's all that really matters."

He smiled, but didn't respond. The death of our parents had changed our lives completely, and we both managed our grief and pain differently. I ran away and started over. Ryan stayed right here and expanded the business beyond what dad could ever have imagined.

"So, what's the plan?" I asked, eager to lighten the mood.

"Let me take your bag to your room. It's the way you left it. I gave strict instructions to the interior designers not to move a thing in case you decide to come back. Of course, you can change the décor if you want to."

"Thank you. But seriously, it's your house and you can change it in any way you want."

His eyebrows twisted, and he positioned his next question carefully. "Does that mean that once you leave, you're not coming back for another eight years?"

Surely I was to blame for him coming to this conclusion. "I'm here, Ryan. I've put my past behind me." I realized that I had to address another topic, and if I was going to do it, I might as well do it now. "Do you remember Mike?"

Confusion colored his face.

"I introduced you two when you visited last summer. Remember?" I asked, trying to jog his memory.

He continued to stare at me, utterly confused.

You have got to be kidding me. "Mike and I are planning to move in together before the fall semester starts. He's starting his doctorate at Harvard. We thought it made sense since Abby is moving to the West Coast with her boyfriend Parker. Please don't tell me you don't remember Abby, either."

"Of course, I remember Abby." He made a face like I had grown two heads. "So, Mike is still your boyfriend, huh? I didn't realize you guys were *that* serious. I looked into him last year. If you were wondering, his record is clean."

"I wasn't," I told him and rolled my eyes. "It didn't even occur to me." *So overprotective.*

"It is important to know everything about the guy you're planning to move in with. What if he's after your money, or he's a serial killer?"

"He is not a serial killer, Ryan. The guy wouldn't hurt a fly. I've known him for almost two years now and he is definitely not after my money because he doesn't even know that I come from money," I assured him. "Thanks to our privately held McAlister Group, people don't really know us very well. Besides, we're not head over heels in love or anything. We're great friends. Our relationship is hassle-free. And seriously, love is so overrated. It only happens in movies, not in real life."

"So…why are you moving in together then?" He squinted his eyes.

"It makes sense if we move in together and see where things go."

I didn't understand why I felt the need to keep convincing him, but I did. "Mike is a nice guy. Abby and Mike have been there for me all these years, and now with Abby leaving I can't think of a better alternative."

"I can." Ryan quickly took the opportunity and said, "Why don't you move back? I can be here for you, if you give me a chance."

"It has nothing to do with you, Ryan. I just don't belong here anymore." There, I had said it. "I want to stay at Harvard and live in Boston with Mike. I'm not sure I can see myself ever living in New York again. Life in Boston is comfortable and safe, and I don't want to give that up."

"Comfort is for when you want to settle down. And love *is* a real thing. Give yourself a chance, Ivy."

"Thank you very much. I'd rather skip this whole love shindig and go straight to comfort."

Mike was always good to me. And good *for* me. The whole love and passion thing, though? I didn't want to go there.

"Fine, if that's what you want. But he has to move into your apartment and not the other way around."

Before I could say another word, Ryan added, "It's not up for a debate."

I nodded with a hint of irritation. *Absolutely great.*

Now I would have to explain to Mike why we get to live in a luxury apartment rent-free. Abby and I had made up a story about how we won some lottery and got to live in this beautiful brand-new building without paying a cent. People never questioned it, but said people also didn't live with me. Mike wasn't going to buy it for long, if he was going to buy it at all.

"I guess that's that," said Ryan. "Go get changed. I made a reservation at Le Balthazar. After lunch, I'll drop you off on Fifth Avenue and head to the hotel to check on the event's preparations."

"Sounds good. I can take a cab back. What time do we have to be at the hotel?" I couldn't be more grateful for the change in the topic.

"Seven. I'll pick you up at six thirty if you think you'll be ready by then."

"That's perfect." I headed toward my room, imagining which designer store I should go to first.

"Ivy, we still need to discuss the business."

"No, we don't." I turned on my heel. "The business is all yours to handle, Ryan. The trust fund Dad left me is more than enough. Not to mention the money you keep transferring into my account every month. Seriously, you don't have to do that."

"That will not work, little sis. You're old enough to take on some of the responsibility. And that trust fund is peanuts when the entire McAlister Group belongs to both of us. I'm not telling you to quit school. I'm telling you to get involved. If you do an internship, do it at our company. That way, in a few years you can join me."

Ryan didn't look too happy with my plans, and I didn't like the turn of our conversation. I had no intention of joining the McAlister Group and I'd made that decision a long time ago. Discussing that with Ryan was a different story altogether.

I made my choice. "Do you mind if we table this discussion for another day? I don't want to ruin your mood. Like you said, today is an important day." I playfully waved at him, turned on my heel again, and dashed to my bedroom. "Christian Dior and Le Balthazar are both waiting for me."

"You're not leaving the city before we talk this out!" Ryan's muffled voice reached me from the hallway.

One thing was obvious: this trip would not be as easy as I had hoped.

Chapter 2

I grabbed the ringing phone and put it on speaker. "Sorry I missed your earlier call, Mike. I got busy." It was true.

It was almost six, and I was running late. Multitasking was the name of the game.

"That's okay," Mike said. *"I wanted to make sure you landed safely."*

I slid the phone onto my vanity and sat down to put on the brand-new mascara that I had learned how to apply properly that afternoon. Thanks to the kind makeup artist at the store who saw me struggling with the tester and gave me a full crash course, so I wouldn't have raccoon eyes an hour into the party.

"Yes, I did land safely. Thank you for checking." I fluttered my eyelashes a few times in quick succession. Turns out I wasn't half bad at this makeup thing.

Abby, you'll be so proud of my newfound artistic abilities.

I never really owned much makeup before. It wasn't my thing. Clothes and accessories…now we're talking. I stood up and twirled in my new gown, liking what I saw. Fashion was my thing.

"I miss you."

Mike's words stopped me in my tracks. I put the mascara wand down on the vanity so I could give the conversation my full attention. "Sorry. I should've called you as soon as I got to New York."

"No worries. You went home for the first time after so many years. I don't expect you to think about me the second you land."

Caring, understanding, and supportive. Who needs love and passion when you have everything else going right in a relationship?

"I can't wait for you to come back to kick off our apartment search. Do you want me to get a head start?" Mike asked enthusiastically.

"Yeah, about that…"

"You changed your mind?"

"What? No. Nothing like that, Mike, I'm ready. Let's look into it together, okay?"

Once he had agreed, somewhat reluctantly, and fell silent, I took the chance to change the subject. "What are your plans for the evening?"

"I'm staying in tonight. Heading to Stamford early tomorrow to see my parents. Not much free time, though. Looks like Patrick will keep me busy this summer."

He made it sound like it was a bad thing, but I knew better. He loved working for Professor Patrick Townsend.

We spoke some more until I heard Ryan's voice in the living room. I promised Mike that I would call him tomorrow and got off the phone.

Hot pink lipstick, here I come!

Our limo pulled up in Midtown, it was impossible to recognize the place even though I'd been there a thousand times. My parents, when they were still alive, were part of the President's

Council of the New York Library that stood across the street from where I was today. I'd spent hours and hours in this area, but never under such circumstances.

A red carpet covered the curb. Event staff directed foot traffic. The walkway was crowded with guests waiting to get in to MoxTo. Bouncers stood by the doors, checking invitations. The place seemed straight out of a movie. I was awestruck, and that was putting it mildly. And the name was quite fitting—an old slang for energy. That was exactly what I felt the moment I stepped through the double doors.

Ryan escorted me toward the lobby through the main entrance. The sublime five-star hotel oozed opulence and offered all the luxuries money could afford. As soon as we entered, flashes started going off all around me. That was not uncommon for Ryan, but it was quite jarring for me. I wasn't part of this glitzy world anymore.

Apprehensively, I turned my back to the cameras.

"You okay?" Ryan asked. His eyes were filled with concern.

"I didn't sign up for *this*." I shielded my eyes from the bright camera flashes.

His loud chuckle didn't help the unease in my stomach. "Relax. One of the biggest annual galas is happening a few blocks away and it's crawling with celebrities. Even if we make it into some small paper, you and I won't be on the front page. These pictures probably won't even make it to the editor's desk."

But there was nothing *small* about New York City as far as I could tell, newspapers included. One picture of me in the paper and I could lose my anonymity. My intention tonight was for everyone to see me with Ryan. So, keeping my inhibition at bay, I wrapped my arm around his and then posed, hoping what Ryan said was true.

Ryan dressed to the nines in a perfect tuxedo. Wearing a coppery silk gown and bright pink chandelier earrings, I didn't look too shabby myself. Our resemblance was obvious: blue eyes, oval faces, and sharp features. We were strikingly similar in so many ways. The only difference was that I was a long-hair brunette, thanks to mom's side of the family, and Ryan had inherited dad's sandy hair. He was fit, and although I didn't hit the gym often, my long runs kept me in great shape.

The hot pink designer heels that somewhat matched my earrings added a few inches to my five-seven frame. I found a perfect match in the showroom, but they were open sandals that did nothing to cover the scar on my left ankle. I had no shame about flaunting my scar, but I wasn't willing to share the story behind it. It was my story, and I wanted to keep it private. The twenty-four hours I shared with Nick were mine and mine only.

"You're doing great," Ryan said, as we smiled at the cameras.

I played cool, so Ryan would stop worrying about me. "I'm in your world, Ryan. I'll do it for you. Don't think my friends read the New York papers, anyway." I waited until the last picture was snapped and I had his full attention. "By the way, did I ever tell you I love you? I'm happy to see you achieving so much. Dad would be so proud of you if he was here today."

"Thanks, sis." Ryan put a hand over my shoulder blade and led me into an open elevator. "Taber and Nick are already upstairs. Without them, this hotel would've never happened."

"What?"

He gave me a puzzled look. "MoxTo is one of our joint ventures. Did I not tell you?"

My stomach kept sinking as the elevator rose, taking us to the highest floor and to the man I never thought I would see again. Nick's memories were sealed deep in my subconscious for years. I had to put them there on purpose, otherwise I would've spent every night thinking about him and his enticing eyes.

Yeah, right!

The sole occupant of your thoughts, whether near or far. The object of your desire. Nick is the only one.

All that time we had spent together… talking and listening… arguing and laughing. Our shared moments and unforgettable happy times, as well as all the painful ones. The butterflies that fluttered in my stomach every time he looked at me.

And then there were his touches… they were electric.

I had tried to feel that same spark with every guy I had met since, but I never did. I looked for a deep connection, which I couldn't find. As time passed, it was easier to give up and accept the reality of life.

I had Mike now and, sparks or not, he was the right person for me. The feelings I had for Nick were a figment of my imagination. I was young and my body was going through changes. Whatever I had felt were only teenage fantasies fueled by hormones.

Lost in thought, I didn't even notice when Ryan and I reached the main hall. And now that I was here, I was completely lost and a bit overwhelmed. Ryan was still beside me, thankfully.

He had to go mingle with the guests. After all, this was his party. So, I straightened my back and decided to brave the scene on my own. There's a first time for everything, right?

"Ryan, you can go talk to people. I can handle being on my—" I couldn't finish my sentence, because I had just noticed Taber and Nick on the other side of the hall.

Nick noticed me, too.

Jeez! The sight of him knocked the air out of me. I felt the power of his gaze from across the room and took a step back to collect myself. The butterflies in my stomach returned with a vengeance. Interesting—I thought they left my body way back when.

This can't be happening to me. I'm twenty-two-and-a-very-freaking-half years old. I'm over letting him make me feel this way.

Taber waved when he spotted Ryan and me, but Nick stood still with his eyes fixated on me. Finally, Taber nudged him and they both started walking toward us.

It was hard to ignore Nick's dominating presence. The crowd parted, giving him space. As much as I tried to, I couldn't take my eyes off of him.

If he was hot back then, he was smoking hot and gorgeously sexy now. With his black tux tailored to his body, accentuating his broad shoulders, lean torso, and long legs, he once again took my breath away. His light brown hair was shorter now. His long nose, sculpted lips, and prominent chin cleft were exactly how I remembered them.

Does he still have those faint dimples on his cheeks when he smiles? Oh, gosh. Stop.

Overall, his features looked harder, stronger, and a lot more mature compared to how I remembered him from four years, five months, and thirteen days ago, but who was counting…

All six-foot-three inches of him had a commanding presence. He carried an authoritative look on his face that screamed *I own this place.*

Duh! He does own it.

"Hey, guys! Look who graced us with her presence today," Ryan announced, bringing me out of my trance.

"Happy to see you, Ivy. Ryan misses you a lot," Taber said.

His warm voice calmed my ragged nerves. Blond facial hair intensified the hues of his blue eyes. Still ruggedly handsome, Taber hadn't changed much in all these years.

"Good seeing you as well, Taber. Looks like congratulations are in order for the success of MoxTo. It's beautiful. And what a great location," I responded with a smile, admiring the way that, after so many years, Ryan, Taber, and Nick were still close.

The venue was full of celebrities. Even the mayor of New York was here—some small party, huh? After a few more minutes of chatting and people-watching, Ryan got pulled aside and Nick and Taber got wrapped up in a discussion about MoxTo that I didn't understand. With nothing else to do, I listened and tried to decipher whatever I could.

My world differed from theirs. People I knew in Boston were not like the ones who surrounded me tonight. I wasn't this person, either.

"Did you find out more about the letter? Does Xavier know?" Taber asked Nick. Hearing them mention Nick's father's name caught my attention.

"No, I don't want him to worry yet. Still trying to figure things out."

My stomach flipped when I heard Nick's deep, sexy voice. Whatever they were talking about, they both seemed concerned.

"What about Ryan and Jonah?" Taber asked.

I didn't mean to eavesdrop, but I also had nowhere to go. Truth was, these were the only people I knew at this party.

"I'll call Jonah later tonight. It's not a good time to discuss it with Ryan," Nick said.

His voice... My heart beat a million miles an hour in his presence. I glanced at everything and everyone but Nick, trying hard to make sure that no one noticed until Taber cleared his throat and got my attention. "So, Ivy, when did you come back?"

"I landed this morning," I answered, with a smile that I hoped hid my quivering lips.

I have liked Taber since I was a kid. He was a mix of Star-Lord's wit and blond hair and the good looks of Thor. He knew how to carry himself and how to win people over. His sister was one of my closest friends. I hadn't seen her, either, for many years.

"That's good to hear. I hope you stop by MoxTo whenever you're in the city. Don't forget to check out Three6T. It's a revolving restaurant just one level below us and is a highlight of this place."

"Sounds amazing. I'll check it out before I leave."

"Want me to make a reservation for you and your friends?" Taber asked.

I laughed awkwardly. Not only did I not know anyone at this party, but I currently didn't know anyone in the city, either. Thankfully, Taber didn't pursue the topic further. We moved on to talking about other things.

Soon I realized that Nick hadn't said a word to me this entire time. In fact, he had not acknowledged my presence, even though I was standing right next to him. Worst of all, he never looked at me from the time he joined me and Ryan. Not once.

And that's how I knew I didn't belong here anymore. Not ever. Never.

No matter how old I was, these men, and most importantly, the man who insisted on ignoring me, would only ever see me as Ryan's little sister and nothing more.

Ryan never came back. Taber excused himself to speak to other guests, which left me and Nick all by ourselves. Talking to the man in my fantasies was easy, but in real life, his presence was nothing short of unnerving.

Another minute went by. He still hadn't initiated a conversation. "Hi," I finally said, taking the reins.

"Hi," was his monosyllabic answer.

That's all I get? It left me incredulous. "I didn't see Jonah. Is he here?" I asked about their fourth friend.

"He's in Vegas. Mostly works from there."

"I see." I didn't understand why; but as awkward as this was, I needed to keep this conversation going. "You look well."

"I guess you can say that."

There were many questions that I wanted to ask, yet I didn't want to know anything about him. Some feelings were better off staying dormant. I was over my heartache. My one-sided love story had already withered away and there was no point in resurrecting it.

Before long, I had no time to reflect on my emotional state because people started joining us. I was being introduced to every person at this party as "Miss Ivy McAlister from the McAlister Group" and "Ryan's sister." Apparently, those were my two identities, as far as Nick was concerned.

I went along. Not that I had a choice. Not that either of those were false.

I shook hands with a very stylish couple in edgy all-white suits. Before I could properly speak to them, Nick pulled me aside. "You should meet Gwen."

The feeling of his fingers encircling my elbow and the spark of his touch took me by surprise. Our eyes met. A high-voltage current ran through my veins. Instinctively, I pulled my arm away.

Is this my imagination, or do I see something in his eyes, too? That very same thing I've been trying to forget for years?

I followed Nick until we stopped beside the profile of a lady in a burgundy sequined gown. She was in a deep conversation with a man I didn't know.

"Gwen, this is Ivy." Nick cut into their private conversation. "She's living in Boston at the moment, not too far from where you are."

He knows where I live? Before I could ask, Gwen turned to face me. As soon as she did, the polite greeting I was about to utter got stuck in my throat. "Oh… Professor Sinclair, it's such…such an honor to meet you in person," I stuttered. Literally.

I was thrilled. Ecstatic, actually, to even stand in front of Professor Gwen Sinclair. Not just respect or admiration—to me; she was a literal scholarly goddess. She was classy, she was beautiful, and she was my role model.

"Hello, Nicholas. Ivy, it's a pleasure to meet you." She extended her hand to me.

I shook it with excitement, like a five-year-old meeting Mickey Mouse for the first time. You could've put me right on a Disney poster with balloons in one hand and an ear-to-ear smile plastered on my face.

"The pleasure is all mine. I've admired you for years." With excitement buzzing in my bones, I couldn't stop talking.

"Is that so? I didn't know I was that famous," she chuckled.

"I've been to all of your seminars in the last couple of years. I'm also joining your class this fall."

"You're a student at Harvard?"

"Yes, I am," I said, beaming.

"I'm so sorry to be the bearer of bad news, then. But due to some unexpected events, I'll be teaching at Columbia this fall."

"Oh. . ." I blinked several times. It was a bombshell I had not expected. Still trying to process how that was possible, I said, "I enrolled in the business program solely because I wanted to be in your class."

"Who was your professor last semester?"

"I had Professor Baldacci," I said, unable to hide the disappointment I felt. "Do you know him?"

"Know him? We're part of the same associations and also very close friends. If you took his class and passed, you must be one of the brightest students in the school."

"Thank you. I try to be in his good books." I went with modesty.

"Wait a minute. Are you Ivy McAlister, by any chance?" Both of her eyebrows shot up. If she was friends with Professor

Baldacci, they must have discussed me by now, since I was the only one moving from his class into Professor Sinclair's. Had he said something about my final assignment?

In my head, I ran through all the assignments I had submitted from my elementary school days all the way to the one I'd submitted a few weeks ago.

Gosh, stop being so dramatic! You were at the top of your class. Even your last project is already in the implementation phase at the customer's site. She didn't bring it up because she thinks you did an awful job.

Professor Sinclair kept staring at me. I couldn't talk. It took me a few more moments to realize that I hadn't answered her question.

Nick jumped in before I could bring myself to speak. "Yes, she is Ivy McAlister. The one and only."

The professor parted her burgundy lips, a shade that perfectly matched her gown; but just then, someone called her name. "Seems like I'm being summoned," she said. "Will you be in the city next week, Ivy?"

"Yes, I'll be here all of next week."

"Good. Here's my card." She handed me a Columbia card with her cellphone number written on the back. "Come see me on Monday."

Confused, I took it and kept staring at it, all the while trying to process this sudden turn of events. By the time I looked up, she was gone.

"You must've made a good impression at Harvard." Nick glanced at the card in my hand.

"That, or my last project was a disaster and she wants to tell me to try harder again." I was mortified. Her moving out of Harvard wasn't sitting well with me, either.

Note to self: Call Blue Chip Corporation to see how the implementation of my project is going.

"You've got very little confidence in yourself." He began walking away and then stopped. "Are you coming, or what?"

When I hesitated, still processing the conversation I had with Professor Sinclair, Nick came back to where he had left me. "Let's get you out of here."

Chapter 3

We reached the bar, a lavish and sophisticated space adorned with architectural finesse, rich mahogany furniture with plush velvet cushions, and soft carpet throughout the room that gave the bar a royal vibe. A floor-to-ceiling glass partition separated us from the open terrace outside. I paid attention to every little detail, trying to keep my sanity in check after the run-in with Professor Sinclair.

Unfortunately for me, it wasn't working.

People around us were busy getting a tour of the hotel and its amenities. With no intention of coming back here again, I skipped the tour altogether.

"Here, drink this. It'll help." Nick handed me a cosmopolitan. This time, I made sure our fingers didn't touch.

As the liquor settled in my stomach, I felt the buzz. My nerves were frayed, and the drink was delicious; it was a sweet, fruity, glorious cascade of flavor.

It had to be a *day*. First, the bombshell Professor Sinclair dropped on me. It also didn't help that I was standing next to the man of my dreams… the man who still haunted me, even though so much time had passed and so much of my life had changed.

A moment alone with Nick. Wasn't this the exact thing I'd always dreamed of?

"Take it easy with the alcohol. You still have a whole evening ahead of you," Nick warned, but I wasn't listening. Instead, I gave the bartender a nod and a second cosmo appeared in front of me.

Liquor undoubtedly helped with my jitters around Nick, but there were certainly pros and cons to drinking alcohol. It calmed my nerves, but it could also make me too bold and more likely to do stupid things that I would later regret.

Being bold around Nick probably wasn't the best idea.

Unless it was.

Absolutely not.

Who am I kidding?

I have a boyfriend now.

My brain and heart kept fighting one another while I continued to gaze at him through my lashes. I wasn't even the slightest bit drunk, but it also didn't mean I was sober. The effect Nick had on me wasn't making the state I was in any better.

His eyes weren't on me any longer, as I would've hoped. He swept the surrounding space with his gaze, seemingly uninterested in the grandeur.

Does he want me to leave and go bother someone else, now that he's handed me the drink? After all, he seems to have lost interest in introducing me to more people.

What else can I expect him to do? Enjoy my company?

Shit, why do I doubt myself so much when I'm around him?

Taking a moment to calm myself down, I decided to ask.

"Bummer." He beat me to it.

"Hmm?"

"It appears someone's perfect plan fell apart."

I masked my feelings for him with disinterest. "What do you know about my perfect plan?"

"I don't need to be a shrink to interpret your reaction. Even Gwen noticed it. You're disappointed that she's leaving."

I rolled my eyeballs and feigned boredom to get him off my back.

"How is New York?" he asked. "Treating you well, I hope."

"New York is boring. And the people here even more so."

"People, or just one person?" He gazed into my eyes, and the charge thickened automatically… if it had ever dissipated.

Instead of responding, I took my phone out of my clutch and emailed Blue Chip for my peace of mind.

Noticing that I was ignoring him, Nick kept throwing questions my way. "What is so interesting about Boston, anyway?"

"The people, I guess," I answered, without looking at him.

"They can't be *that* great. Try again. You can do better than that."

"What's with the interrogation? Is there no one else here you can talk to?"

I scowled. He raised his hands in surrender.

I was only halfway through my email to Andy, the project manager at Blue Chip, when Nick's laugh filled my ears. Exhaling, I raised my eyes to meet his.

"Relax. Your project was impressive. I'm pretty sure that's not the reason Gwen changed universities."

I glanced at my email and then back at him again. "How do you know so much about Professor Sinclair and my project?"

"Let's just say I know a thing or two more than you."

His words didn't explain a thing, and it wasn't like I could ask a follow-up question because a visitor interrupted us. He was a man of my height with a big camera in hand.

"Hi. My name's Cooper," he said. "I'm covering the MoxTo opening." He raised his camera to further indicate his job. "Mind if I take a picture of you two and ask you a few questions, Miss McAlister?"

My demeanor changed, which Nick didn't take long to notice. "No pictures tonight," he told Cooper. With a hand on my back, Nick ushered me away from the reporter. "What's wrong?"

"I don't want my pictures to come out," I told him.

He laughed wretchedly. "This is the wrong place to be if you don't want your picture taken. You realize that, right?"

"I clearly made a mistake by coming." My irritation flared. Ryan was *so* getting it!

"I'll see what I can do to keep them out of the press."

And just like that, we were back to our old routine of bicker, rinse, and repeat.

We reached the open terrace that overlooked the glamorous bustling enigma that was Times Square. The view from this level brought back such fond memories of my old life here. I've changed so much since I left, but the city was still the same. It made me wonder if I truly missed living here or if it was a passing phase.

Abby's move, and learning that Professor Sinclair had transferred to Columbia, left me untethered. I gave myself a week to decide what I was going to do with my life, since my old plans had just been shattered right in front of my eyes.

Right now, though, I had other things on my mind. Rather, the only thing.

I chose not to dwell on that thought, either. I wanted to enjoy the beauty of this place and bask in nostalgia, instead of thinking of the man who still took my breath away as though no time at all had passed.

Sipping my drink, I moved away slightly, all the while trying to act like he didn't affect me in the slightest. I was buzzing in more ways than one.

Leaning over the glass parapet, I peered down. There were still so many people in the streets below, many trying to enter MoxTo. I supposed everyone wanted to find out what the hype was all about.

None of those people mattered more than Nick, who appeared next to me again. The surrounding air was charged with a thick undercurrent that was hard to ignore. I concentrated on my breathing and waited for my heart to calm down, but all I breathed in was his intoxicating scent. Bergamot and sage, and so utterly Nick that my heart beat unsteadily as if pulsing for him.

Nick! Nick! Nick! Why did he feel like home? In my world, he *was* my home.

"Do you know where Ryan went? Haven't seen him in a while." I needed to talk about something else—something that didn't revolve around us. A distraction, maybe some space. I needed… I needed *him*.

Our gazes locked. My heart stopped. I couldn't break eye contact no matter how much I tried. He tugged me toward him with unexplainable force, like he was the very thing I orbited around.

Lost in his eyes, I had forgotten my question by the time I heard him say, "No. I don't know where Ryan is."

My body craved his touch. Something—*anything*. Were his lips as soft as I had imagined? How would it feel to be kissed by Nick, since I'd only ever kissed him in my fantasies. Would he live up to my expectations, or were fantasies always more satisfying than reality?

His eyes wouldn't leave mine. I wanted to know what was going on in his head. Did he think the same as me? Did he feel the longing? The need?

My heartbeat quickened when he took a step closer. He was mere inches away.

When the back of his fingers brushed the length of my arm, I instinctively looked down at where my skin burned. A tremor ran through my body. One more of these touches and I swear I would go into cardiac arrest.

Pulling my chin up with his index finger, he waited until our eyes met again. "You feel that, too, don't you?"

His deep voice vibrated through me. The world around us vanished into a black hole, leaving only me, Nick, and this moment.

I feel it. Of course I do. How can I not when it's you who's touching me?

I froze, silent as a statue, filled with anticipation as to what he would do.

Nick took another step toward me, close enough that we touched chest to chest. I breathed in the scent of his aftershave once again. He smelled divine. Without taking his eyes off of me, Nick took the glass out of my hand and set it down on a nearby table. He put his hands around my waist and pulled me closer, if that was even possible. There was nowhere to go, even if I wanted to escape. My breaths came shorter and my heart threatened to burst out of my chest.

"You haven't changed a bit in all these years," he murmured, bending down so his lips brushed my ear.

A tingle shot through my belly. I shuddered in the circle of his embrace. His warm breath on my neck made me achingly aware that I wasn't dreaming as his lips caressed my cheek. And then, slowly, almost torturously, he brushed his mouth against mine.

It started as a slow seductive kiss, like carefully dipping into the water to check its temperature. It tantalized my senses and awakened all of my desires. The kiss was almost chaste, almost hesitant, until the gentleness ebbed and he deepened it into something that matched the intensity of what we both felt.

My whole body was alight. He torched every nerve ending. The only thing reverberating in my head was his name, as every need in my body responded to his kiss.

Yet I found myself holding back. Maybe I was using my dreams as a reference point, trying to figure out if this kiss was meeting my expectations. Or maybe I was in complete seductive shock, if there even was such a thing, because the actual kiss was a million times more potent than I'd ever imagined it could be.

People milled around us with their stares burning a hole in my back, but I didn't care. Nick ran his fingers through my hair before cupping my face and holding me in place.

I parted my lips for him. His tongue swept into my mouth, taking the lead, and I relinquished any semblance of control up to him. His tongue explored me, probed me, taking what he wanted from me. I willingly offered everything up.

Sliding my hands under his suit jacket, I wrapped them around his waist. Even through his dress shirt and vest, I could feel the heat radiating from his body and seeping into mine. His hard muscles rippled under the palm of my hands, and there was only one thought in my head.

I want more.

Soon I was kissing him back passionately, my tongue meeting his. Tangling and deepening the kiss, I matched his intensity. My skin burned with desire and my body craved more. My hands roamed up his back, trying to feel every inch of the hard muscles. The layers of clothing couldn't keep us at bay.

Neither the crowd nor the public place could hold our burning desire in check. I was desperate to touch his bare skin and feel it against mine.

I wanted Nick. Badly.

He pulled me into him like he couldn't stand even an inch of distance between us. The dull ache that started when we met this evening had turned into an unbearable throbbing pain between my legs.

I didn't know who pulled away first, but at some point we broke apart. I didn't know how long we had been kissing, but it didn't seem long enough.

Moving away, I tried to bring my breathing back to normal. He was breathless, too. I wondered whether his brain was as fuzzy as mine.

In twenty-two years, I had never experienced such an intense kiss. It left me swathed in passion and with the need for another. He had that power over me, over my body. I always knew that when the moment came, I would be powerless in front of him.

Moving further away, I slowly started coming to my senses. He was quiet and I was speechless. Another minute went by. Once the physical contact we relished withered away, I came back to earth and realized I wasn't that kid who salivated over my teenage crush. I was someone else now. I had a boyfriend now.

Guilt immediately overtook me. Shame slid icy fingers down my spine, nestling in my gut. My instinct was to hide, but I didn't know where to go, what to do, or what to make out of the situation I had gotten myself into. All I understood was that I had to make this right with Nick and with Mike, who was unaware of anything.

"I'm so sorry, Nick. I got carried away. This shouldn't have happened."

He tugged me closer, holding my wrist, and like a broken leaf I swayed toward him. I had no control over my body or my senses—that was the power he still had over me.

Back away.

But I couldn't. His presence had me captivated. This was *right*. It had to be.

Nick's fierce eyes held mine before his lips parted. "No. You're not sorry. I know I'm not."

I had to tell him this was a mistake. He might be available, but I wasn't, and I had to make that crystal clear.

Before I could put an end to this insanity, his finger was on my lips. "Don't ruin this moment, Ivy."

"Nick, listen to me. It's too late."

"It wasn't possible back then," he protested.

"You didn't even try." That definitely wasn't what I meant to say. My reasonable brain had a tendency to shut down around him.

Don't fall into that rabbit hole again, Ivy. Nothing good can ever come out of this. Nick is nothing but bad news and you know it.

"You were a minor," Nick stated.

"As if I would've run to the cops to tell on you."

"That wasn't the point."

"The point is you knew that our age difference never mattered to me. Was it really such a big deal for you?" *Crap!* That was not what I wanted to say, either.

His lips parted to say something. I hoped for the explanation I had been waiting for, but instead someone called out his name and interrupted us. It was a woman who used his full name.

Nicholas.

I pulled away like a kid caught stealing candy from a jar, and we both turned toward the woman's voice.

"Hey, babe! I was searching for you everywhere. Didn't realize this is where you were hiding."

A blonde in a silver gown closed the gap between herself and Nick, and then she wrapped her arms around him and kissed him on the lips.

What the hell? The lips that touched mine belong to her?

Utterly confused, I looked from the woman to Nick and back again. I pulled myself away, putting even more distance between Nick and me.

She was no Celine. Celine was gorgeous and sophisticated. Throughout the years, I'd seen her on many billboards and magazine covers.

A fitting place to be when you are a stunning French supermodel.

This woman, though, was equally gorgeous, but in a more *sexpot* kind of way. Her radiant skin glowed. There was not a single ounce of excess fat and the high slit cut into the bottom of her dress revealed her seemingly never-ending legs. The way she stood made it look like she was posing. Another model, perhaps? Then there were the perfect teeth, perfect smile, perfect nose, bulging tits, long blonde curls…And Nick was screwing her.

I hated her immediately.

"Ivy, this is Mindy," Nick decided to introduce us, breaking the awkward silence. "She is MoxTo's manager. Mindy, this is Ivy. Ryan's sister."

Of course. To Nick, I was only Ryan's sister. Who else could I be?

"Oh, so *you* are Ivy. I've heard so much about you. All good things, of course." She spoke in a raspy voice and added a smile at the end. A fake one, from the looks of it.

She clearly wanted me to know that Nick belonged to her, so she sensuously moved her hands over his back before draping his arm around her shoulders and snuggling against him.

I should leave right now. I don't belong here. What was I thinking when I kissed him? Another figment of my imagination, perhaps?

It couldn't be. I could still feel his touch, his kiss on my lips, and his warm breath on my skin.

Get hold of yourself, Ivy!

Ashamed for letting him play with me like that, I took a few more steps back until I touched the cocktail table behind me and had nowhere else to go.

Nick removed her hands from him, though she didn't seem ready to let go. So, it was a power play to show me that Nick was hers? She must've noticed how close Nick and I were when she approached us. For all I knew, she might've even seen us kissing.

He gave her a stern glare and she let go of his arm.

I tried to understand their dynamic, but I couldn't. *She hates me.* My face burned hot from the mounting embarrassment.

"I'm so glad you came for MoxTo's opening today." She put her hand out to shake mine. "Nice meeting you."

"It was nice meeting you as well, Mindy." With nowhere to run from this situation, I shook her hand while trying hard to conceal the turmoil inside of me.

She was gorgeous and looked perfect standing next to Nick. Completely fake, sure, but perfect. It was infuriating.

"I hope you're planning to stay in the city for a while. I know Ryan would like that very much," Mindy said.

There was no actual reason for me to be upset with her. After all, it wasn't her fault I had the hots for her boyfriend or whatever he was to her. I tried to look at her fingers, but they were locked down in a fist.

"I'm here for a week," I said, trying to sound as civil as I could.

"We'll see," Nick announced to no one in particular. I looked at him, surprised. Mindy did, too.

Nick didn't explain himself. I had a feeling he didn't explain his reasons and motives to others often. He put his hand on Mindy's back and they both headed back inside, leaving me on the terrace all by myself.

Chapter 4

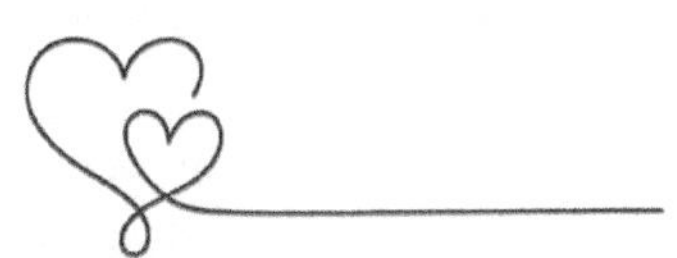

What a stupid fool I was to fall for Nick again! What the hell was I thinking? Did I really think I'd come back here after so many years and find that Nick had waited for me? Hell, he didn't wait for me to begin with. That was the exact reason I stopped going to his parents' house in the first place.

He was nothing more than a teenage fantasy… my first and, sadly, unrequited love. Or maybe it wasn't even love. Maybe it was a big fat crush that I had to forget. Now I had Mike and a life back in Boston. Boston was where I belonged. I had a solid plan. All I had to do was stick to it.

Mindy…

What if Mindy was his fiancée, or worse, his wife? My stomach twisted in knots. Their relationship seemed so strange. But then again, how well did I know them? Not well at all, to be honest. Mindy was a complete stranger, but so was Nick. Since when had I become bold enough to make out with strangers?

But how can Nick be a stranger when I think about him more than I think about myself?

Make up your mind, Ivy.

I halted mid-stride, remembering the half-finished cosmopolitan I left on the terrace. Instead of going back to that god-awful place to grab it, I decided to get a fresh one at the bar.

Once I found a chair, I took off my stilettos and started massaging my achy feet. *Going to events that require uncomfortable footwear—yet another reason I don't belong in this city anymore.*

It wasn't like I never wore stilettos and dresses. Fancy parties with all the unfamiliar faces were not my thing. They never were and never will be.

The bartender must've recognized me from earlier because, before I could order, he handed me another cosmo with a smile. I thanked him and took a big sip before setting the glass down. The alcohol was good for my nerves, but terrible for my aching head.

But sitting on the sidelines and observing people without having to take part in awkward, empty chit-chatting was right up my alley. So, that was what I did: I watched beautiful men and women parading by in their glamorous clothes. I didn't mind this even one bit.

"Ivy? Is that you?"

I turned to the sound of a familiar voice, half-expecting to see a thin, lanky boy. Instead, I met with a tall and confident-looking man with a cute smile and curly black hair.

"Dustin? I'm so happy to see you!" I gave him a genuine, wide smile.

We had been neighbors and friends. We'd even gone to the same school. We had known each other for ages and were much more than close acquaintances. "You look gorgeous," Dustin said.

"Thank you. How have you been?" I asked, excited to meet an actual known person at this party—at least, outside of Taber and Nick and my brother.

He pulled up a bar stool and sat next to me. "I'm doing well. Just finished my undergrad. Next is an MBA before I join my dad in our family business. He wants to make sure I get a couple of years to myself before I do. Once I dive in, there will be no time for relaxing or fun."

"That's great! Happy to see you here. How are your parents? How's Peter?"

Dustin whistled and got more comfortable. "Parents are good. Big bro is already working for Dad," he said. "But tell me about you! Where have you been all this time?"

"I'm still in Boston. I missed Ryan though, so figured I'd come visit for a few days."

We talked for a good while and I brought him up to speed about my education and life. "Are you in touch with anyone from our school group?" I asked, feeling guilty as well as excited.

The last year of middle school had been a disaster. Even though so much time had passed, I had to wonder whether my close circle of friends from back then would embrace me or want nothing to do with me if we met. "I'm really sorry for being a douche that last year I was here," I apologized.

"Don't say that. We all understood what you were going through. Honestly, I don't know what I would've done in that situation. I'm happy to see you back, though." His kind words and genuine smile warmed my insides more than the alcohol.

"How long are you in the city?" he asked. "Let's catch up over the weekend. I'll see if some of them are around."

"I'm here for a week, and that would be really awesome."

"Sweet! We should probably exchange numbers, so we can figure out what time and day works best for everyone."

I took out my phone and was about to hand it to Dustin when I felt Nick's presence. Not sure how I knew it was him. I simply did.

"That won't be necessary," Nick said, rudely intruding on our conversation. "Ivy won't be available this weekend."

A slight touch of Nick's finger made me aware of the fact that he was resting his hand on the back of my chair. I couldn't tell if his touch was intentional, but the butterflies were already flying high in my belly.

Nick is screwing someone else and you have a boyfriend. I heard the silent scold for what felt like the hundredth reminder of this evening. Pushing those gnawing feelings aside, I concentrated on what was happening in front of me.

No way I was going to let Nick jump into a private conversation—our conversation—but Dustin beat me to it. "That's all right. It is kind of short notice, anyway. We can try for next week, Ivy." He turned to Nick and offered his hand. "I'm Dustin, by the way."

"Nicholas." Nick shook his hand without saying another word.

I fought back a laugh. *Uptight, much?*

Despite Nick scowling at me, I handed my phone to Dustin. He saved his number, and then I took my phone back and called *his* phone just to vex Nick further.

"Text me once you hear from everyone," I told Dustin. "Even if no one else can make it, we should catch up in a more casual atmosphere."

In my peripheral vision, I could make out the annoyance on Nick's face. Not that I cared. I was pissed at him far too much.

"We have to leave now. It's getting late," Nick announced.

"Is the party wrapping up? If that's the case, I'll wait for Ryan." I took a sip from my glass. I was borderline worried because I hadn't seen Ryan since the time he'd left me with his friends. It wasn't unlike him, though; we were all part of one big extended family. Or at least that was what Ryan thought.

"He dipped a while back," said Nick.

I almost choked on my drink. "What?"

"Something important came up and he left. He asked me to get you home safe."

I smirked. "There is no way you're taking me home. I can call a cab."

Dustin must've felt the tension and intervened. "I can drop you off at home if you'd like. I'm assuming you're staying at Ryan's, right? That means we're neighbors again, at least for the week."

"So are we," Nick interjected, no longer trying to hide his annoyance. "That won't be necessary. Ivy is my responsibility."

His responsibility? Like hell I am!

"And we meet again." Mindy appeared and possessively wrapped her left arm around Nick's biceps. "Every time I lose Nicholas I search for you, and there he is." She smiled, but it didn't reach her eyes.

If she wanted to embarrass me, she had succeeded. But if she had seen me kissing Nick, I deserved that and more.

Dustin raised one brow at me as if to say, *what's going on with her?* All I could do was ignore her bitchiness and shake my head. "Dustin, this is Mindy. MoxTo's manager." I took it on myself to introduce the two, since Nick showed no interest in introducing Mindy or speaking to Dustin at all.

"Hi. I'm Dustin Hart, Ivy's childhood friend."

"Nice to meet you, Dustin. Are you sure you're just friends? You guys look so cute together," she cooed, and scampered her hand down Nick's forearm.

No ring. A girlfriend, at most. Relief washed over my entire body.

Dustin raised his eyebrows as if to ask what her deal was. I made a face again, letting him know I wasn't sure.

"Need anything?" Nick asked Mindy, his voice downright icy.

"A couple of reporters are waiting in my office. They want to interview you."

He untangled his arm from hers. "Reschedule it for another day."

Her sweet demeanor shifted. "They want to run the story on MoxTo tomorrow and you've been giving them the cold shoulder all week. Let's get it over with. We can leave together."

That last part was meant for me. It had to be. Nick was taken. I got that. Loud and clear.

"Not happening tonight," he said. "Reschedule it."

"But Nick—"

"Do as I say."

That was all she needed to turn on her heel and leave in a huff.

"Ivy, we're leaving," Nick reminded me.

My responsible guardian and the bane of my existence.

I put on my heels and gave Dustin a big hug. "I can't wait to hang out with you later in the week." Then, ignoring Nick, I walked out.

Unfortunately for me, he followed.

I entered the elevator, and so did Nick. Once inside, he reached across his chest and pressed the button for the lobby. The elevator descended.

"You don't need to babysit me. I already told you I can take a rideshare. Clearly, you have important things to do and more important people to be with." I took Mindy's irritation out on him.

The fact that it made me mad was actually a good thing. It was much easier to be around him when I was upset.

"Do I look like a nanny to you?"

As hard as it was, I faced the elevator doors so I didn't have to look at him. "You're definitely acting like one."

Why did you do it? Why did you kiss me after all this time? I wanted to scream the questions in his face. Instead, I remained silent, not sure if I would like the answer.

With every passing second, the air inside the elevator hardened. The only thing that kept me sane was my irritation.

Tonight, I not only realized my feelings for Nick hadn't diminished one bit, but the kiss we shared had only intensified the wants I had hidden for years.

Nothing else mattered because, despite the damned circumstances, the world ceased to exist whenever he was near me. Even his girlfriend's catty comments didn't stop me from wanting him. Our history and our shared past superseded everything.

Seconds ticked by slowly. I was finding it harder to breathe the same air as Nick. All I could smell was his cologne mixed with the scent that was so purely, unmistakably Nick.

God, I was crazy about him. Hypnotized by his scent. Mesmerized by his eyes.

So unhinged that my libido made me forget how wrong it was for me to feel this way. He was in a relationship. I was taken. And yet, I couldn't stop imagining him pulling me closer and kissing me senseless again.

You have no shame.

But that was the thing. I didn't have any shame. All I could think about was Nick, hard and rough, tearing me apart.

We finally reached the lobby and the elevator door opened, I rushed across the marble floors, pushed open the main glass doors, and ran outside so I could breathe again.

A fancy electric blue sedan pulled up to the curb. As soon as the valet handed Nick the keycard, Nick and I reached for the passenger-side door handle at the same time.

"What are you doing?" he asked.

"I can open my door. Besides, I need to maintain some distance," I snapped back.

"Four years wasn't enough?"

"Apparently not." I went for the door handle again.

In complete frustration, he put his hand on the car door and stopped me from getting in. "Whatever you want to say to me, say it."

"What do you want me to say? That you're with Mindy so you should leave me alone? I shouldn't have to tell you that."

"It's not serious."

"You are delusional."

"She means nothing to me."

"Why did you kiss me?"

When he didn't speak, I pushed his hand aside, opened the car door, and got in.

He rounded the back of the car and got in, too. His proximity, and the fact that we were breathing the same air, made me nervous, irritated, and frustrated. But there was another sensation, some undeniable sexual undercurrent, that made me feel like I had no control over myself or the situation I was in.

I had to stay away from Nick. I knew that. But the compelling need to be with him was something I couldn't understand or reason with. A single touch of his hand had the power to melt me into oblivion.

The short drive from the hotel to my house felt like the longest trip I had ever taken. The instant the car slowed down in front of my building, I had one foot out the door before it could make a complete stop.

But in the rush, I ended up struggling to remove my seatbelt. Nick put his hand over mine and stopped me. My skin prickled, reacting to him. I looked down at where our hands connected. He didn't remove his hand, and I didn't pull mine away, either. Lost in the moment, I lifted my gaze to meet his. The burning need in his eyes burned through my skin, like a blazing fire running down my bloodstream.

"Why are you fighting this?" Nick waited for my response, but I couldn't speak. "We can't hide this forever, Ivy. We are going to happen."

He removed his hand, and I bolted out of the car and ran inside my building. As the blood rushed to my ears, all I could hear was his voice, saying, *"We are going to happen."*

Chapter 5

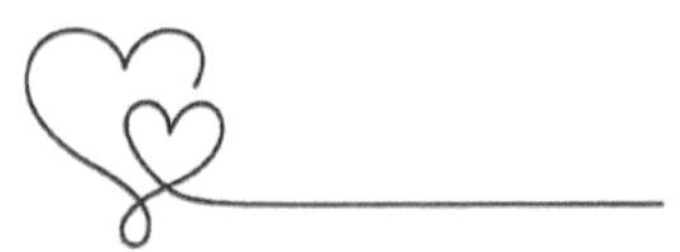

The exchange between Nick and I at the Hampton house was the first of many. I suppose that particular one stood out because it was the first time he noticed me in the same way that I had been noticing him for years.

Even after I left New York, I couldn't stop thinking about him. That single moment we shared was enough to make me want more. A whole lot more.

But Nick being Nick—someone who had tons of options—he never made a move on me.

His parents, Rosanne and Xavier took over being the authority figures Ryan and I were missing in our lives. We loved them dearly, and they loved us as their own. Being orphans, we couldn't have asked for more.

In many ways Rosanne reminded me of my mother, so much so that during those dark days it used to hurt. But I wasn't an ungrateful bitch. Even if I avoided them the entire year, I still went to their house in Woodbury, New York, during the holidays.

Other than spending time with my brother and getting loved on by Rosanne and Xavier, I also wanted to see Nick, the guy who consumed my every dream since I became a teenager. The same guy who never acted on those feelings because I was a kid.

Still, the holidays at Branson home continued to be the highlight of my year.

I missed Nick madly after I moved to Boston. Boys in my school always tried to ask me out, but the feeling wasn't mutual. I never wanted them the way I wanted Nick. My mind was always filled with memories of him. No one got my heart racing the way he did.

During those two weeks I spent at his parents' home, we'd stay up and talk for hours. From the business world to world news, we both had a lot to share. Nick was an attentive listener, and he genuinely cared what I had to say. Our interests and views aligned for most topics, and when they didn't, we debated until one of us proved our point. We joked, made each other laugh, enjoyed outdoor activities, and watched sports together. We exchanged glances and intentionally brushed against each other while passing. On some occasions, we even danced.

As much as I cherished our time and tried to make it last, those two weeks would fly by fast. Despite that, as close as we were, he tried nothing. Not once. Me being too young to know what to do, we'd end up going our separate ways.

In school, I was always the studious one who never looked up from her books. If I wasn't in the school or library, I would hide inside my apartment and watch hours of TV shows.

By the time my senior year of high school rolled around, I had already secured early admission at Harvard University. Like I did every year, I rushed to the Bransons' home on the morning of Christmas Eve, all excited to see everyone and share the good news. I couldn't wait to see Nick's reaction when I told him.

But that wasn't the only thing I planned on sharing with him that day. I came prepared to tell him how I felt about him. The countless nights I stayed awake thinking about him, imagining his lips on mine…I had waited long enough and I was ready to experience it all with him… with the real him this time.

None of the boys showed until late in the afternoon, including Ryan. I was anxious, but I kept it in. I wanted to appear mature and confident when Nick showed up, but as the guests kept filing in, Nick was nowhere to be found.

A delicious dinner appeared on the table. Everyone was seated by the time Nick entered the dining room with a hot blonde on his arm.

Celine, Celine, Celine… The name rang in my ears even though he only said it once.

That was the end of my holidays with Nick and the Branson family, as well as my last Christmas with Ryan.

I wasn't expecting sleep tonight. Every time I closed my eyes; I felt his gaze. His touch, our heated kiss, his warm scent…The onslaught of his tongue inside my mouth kept me up with a need too strong for me to comprehend.

"We can't hide this forever, Ivy. We are going to happen."

What game was he playing? What the hell was I thinking? I was in New York for a week and then going back to where I belonged. I had a boyfriend, and we were planning to move in together. My friends were in Boston. I only came back for Ryan; to accept my past and to tell him I was there for him. To show him I wasn't the same Ivy who ran away from pain. Through therapy, I left all the darkness behind. Broke all the emotional barriers that kept me from being myself. I was a strong woman now.

But was coming back here a giant mistake?

I really thought I had gotten over Nick. But clearly I hadn't, because after spending a few moments in his presence, I once again felt drawn to him. Like all the years of growing and healing had been in vain… like my world without Nick didn't exist.

The thoughts of him consumed me… of his body on top of mine, of his tongue in my mouth, of his hands touching me in all those places I had always wanted him to touch.

I wasn't strong, by any definition of the word. I was a wreck.

By five a.m. I gave up on the idea of sleep altogether, changed into my shorts and sports bra, and went for a run. I had always found running helpful, even in the middle of unrealistic deadlines at school and university. All I could hope for was that a strenuous run followed by a cold shower would help me function like a normal human being.

After a two-hour run in my lush and beloved Central Park, I came home refreshed and ready to take on the day. For once, there were no thoughts of Nick in my head. All my brain could process was the soreness in my muscles and the unnaturally hot temperature.

Whoever said that global warming wasn't real was a fool.

I removed my Bluetooth earbuds and dropped them on the kitchen counter. I pulled my phone out of my pocket to turn off the music, and that was when I noticed one unread message from Abby.

Hi girlfriend. How is NYC? And how is the sexiest man in the country treating you?

I rolled my eyes but couldn't stop laughing. Abby had had a crush on Ryan years ago. That was until she met Parker. Now she called Ryan "the sexiest man in the country" as a joke.

I got to typing. **Ew! Can we not refer to my brother as the sexiest man in the country? He has been MIA. Btw, I need to tell you something. Can I call?**

Nobody else knew about my one-sided teenage crush on Nick. After last night, I couldn't keep it to myself either. Abby was direct and non-judgmental, like a sister I'd never had. If there was anyone in the world I could discuss this with, it was her.

I wasn't a woman to cheat on my boyfriend. The guilt was eating me alive. But what I felt for Mike, or what I might've felt for any other guy in the past, didn't compare to my deep, albeit unrequited feelings for Nick. I had to talk it all out, or I was going to explode.

A minute later, a message popped up on my screen. *It's a crazy day at the office. Is it okay if I call you tomorrow?*

Why are you working on a weekend? Her job at a law firm paid well and helped her cover all of her expenses, but her bosses clearly had no boundaries.

I'm on deadlines to wrap up some projects. Taking Sunday and Monday off, though. Will call as soon as I can.

There went my chance to confess, what a crummy girlfriend I was. **Take care of yourself. Talk soon.**

I was going to the kitchen to pour myself a glass of water, all the while trying to think of anything other than Nick, when the doorbell rang. With a heavy sigh I turned to walk to the door, ready for a full-blown grown-up conversation with my brother that, to be frank, was long overdue.

I opened the door. "I should've played a prank on you and changed the locks for leaving me at your party last—" I stopped as soon as I realized it wasn't Ryan standing there.

How could it be? Why would he ring the doorbell when he lives here, you dummy?

I moved aside and let Nick in. "I wasn't expecting you." Closing the door, I followed him into the kitchen. He set two cups of coffee and a brown to-go box that smelled of bagels on the counter.

Why is he here? Why isn't he letting me forget him?

"If you weren't expecting me, then why do you smell sexy so early in the morning?"

"Seriously?" I gawked at his taut back in front of me.

He glanced over his shoulder and winked at me; a wink that made me stop in my tracks.

A devilish glint played in his eyes that I hadn't seen in years. Throw in an irresistible, heart-melting dimple that only came to life when he smiled, and I was officially doomed.

"Just got back from a run." I tried to regain some control over the conversation. Placing my palms on the edge of the counter, I hoisted myself up and pushed an annoying strand of loose hair behind my ear.

I couldn't help but be aware of how terrible I must've smelled compared to him and his freshly washed body, his bergamot cologne, and his pheromones.

"You are beautiful no matter what," he said, not even trying to hide the fact that he was checking me out.

"I have a boyfriend." I blurted it out before my mind got foggy from his presence.

"Interesting." He didn't even flinch. "Trying to level the ground?"

I rolled my eyes. "It's a fact. And unlike you, he means something to me."

"Are you sure about that?"

I decided not to take the bait. My body, however, wasn't so easily convinced. I couldn't look away. The man was a different level of hot.

"Do you work out every day? I'm guessing you have a personal trainer." I asked mainly to change the subject.

Judging from how good his body looked, he probably lived at the gym.

"You want to join? My trainer can train us together." He hit me with another one of his over-the-top smiles. I couldn't help but flash back to last night and the way his fiery green eyes wanted me… and how they'd been filled with desire…

This was bad. Terrible. The last thing I wanted was for history to repeat itself. "Why are you here? And where is Ryan?"

It worked. The flirty glint in his eyes disappeared immediately. "That's why I'm here. To take you to Ryan. Got you some coffee and your favorite breakfast. Hope it's still your favorite. You can take a shower and pack." He peeked at his watch and added, "We need to leave in exactly one hour."

It took me a while to understand what he said because I was too busy ogling him. His dark-blue T-shirt molded itself to his body, accentuating his muscular torso, the ridges of his pectorals, and his bulging biceps. I tried to stop myself before he caught me, but when it came to Nick, I was absolutely powerless.

"Pack what? Where are we going?"

"Clothes, Ivy. Where we're going, you need to wear clothes." His smug face vexed me.

His eyes weren't ready to leave me. He was still smiling and gloating because he knew he had this effect on me. And he was enjoying himself completely.

Desperate to break our staring contest, I turned and left for the shower; but it didn't mean that I'd let him win.

The cold shower washed away all my lingering desires. I changed into a white cotton sundress that accentuated my meager curves. This would have to do—after all, since I didn't know where we were going, I had no idea what to wear or what to pack.

I didn't bother doing my hair or makeup, either. If these clothes were all I had to wear, that was what Nick would get.

I followed the fresh smell of bagels and found Nick sitting at the breakfast table. Feeling much better now that I had told him about Mike, I took the chair beside him. Nick was my brother's best friend. It wasn't like I could ignore him or pretend he didn't exist. We had to be civil with each other, for Ryan's sake.

"How did you know I take my coffee strong and black?" I asked, after he slid a cup toward me and smiled. "And these bagels are from my favorite bakery in the city. I haven't had an authentic New York bagel in years." I took a big bite out of my toasted bagel with smoked salmon, avocado, and capers. It was delicious, and exactly the way I remembered New York bagels.

"Where are we going? I'm not sure what to pack," I asked, between bites. "I don't even know if I'm appropriately dressed right now."

"You're perfect. Pack whatever you want. If you're missing something, you can always buy it."

"What is this big mystery? Why can't you tell me where we are going?"

"It's a surprise," he said, and smiled again.

"I hate surprises."

"Trust me. You will love this one."

Chapter 6

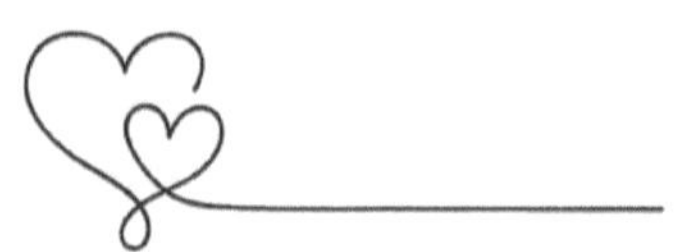

By any other city's standard, it was an early Saturday morning, though it was not too early for New Yorkers and tourists to fill the streets. Street vendors had already set up their stalls, the food vendors were warming up pretzels, and families were walking briskly toward Central Park. A full twenty-four hours hadn't even passed since I got here and, in some ways, I was falling in love with this city's vibe once again.

The sun hid behind dark clouds as we started our drive in Nick's bright yellow Lamborghini. Despite the foot traffic, there wasn't a lot of car traffic to stall us.

A colossal weight had fallen off of my chest now that he knew I wasn't available, and I tried to make peace with the fact that he was with Mindy. Things were finally going back to exactly how I wanted them to be.

That kiss from last night? Eventually, I would forget that, too.

Not true, Ivy. You will always remember that kiss because no one has ever kissed you like that before. Besides, you would prefer him to be naked and all over you, but you're too scared to make it a reality.

"Are we going on this trip so you can show off your car collection?" I asked, trying to both strike up a conversation and get a grip over my internal undulation.

He laughed. "What, you don't like this car? I prefer gas cars for trips to the countryside. Better safe than sorry."

"Aha! So we *are* going to the countryside. I guess it's time to play Twenty Questions."

He set his eyes back on the road. "No."

"It's against the rules to give monosyllabic answers."

"Good. We're not playing any games. Some surprises are worth the wait." And that was the end of that conversation.

Or so he thought. "How did you know about my project with the Blue Chip?" I asked.

"I already told you: We're not playing Twenty Questions." His lips twitched a bit.

Clearly, he was only pretending to be annoyed, so I pushed further. "No problem. One answer to one question will do."

He stared at me through the red light, deciding whether or not to answer. When the light turned green, he faced the road again. "Fine," he said. "I own Blue Chip."

I almost jumped in my seat. "Are you serious? I did a ton of research on the company. Your name never came up. Neither did Branson Capital."

"What can I say? Either you're not good at research, or I'm good at hiding things." His lips twitched again, mocking me. He clearly enjoyed riling me up.

Annoyance surged through me, mostly at myself. But I wasn't ready to accept what he was telling me. "I interned at Blue Chip in my senior year and no one ever mentioned you. When did you buy it?"

"I don't know. Maybe a year ago."

In an instant, I went from annoyed to upset. "Did you buy the company because I was interning there?"

He smiled, ignoring my rising anger. "Relax. Don't get a coronary now." He chuckled. "I wasn't running after you."

"I didn't think you were, but that doesn't answer my question."

"You said it would be one question and now we're at how many? Four?" he asked playfully. When he saw my face, he must've decided to put me out of my misery. "I didn't know you interned there. M&A handles these things. I'm not involved in daily activities."

Mergers and Acquisitions didn't fall under daily activity, but I let it go. "How come Branson Capital didn't come up when I was doing my research?"

"I'll tell you, but this is the last answer you will get out of me," he warned. "Branson Capital is the umbrella company. Then we have subsidiaries and branches that work independently. Unless you're a market analyst and are ready to spend all of your time researching or reviewing financials, these things can be hard to find."

That made sense. I would've loved to get a crash course on research from Nick Branson. He'd been in the business world for far too long and clearly had a wealth of knowledge, but he didn't seem in the mood to share.

Once my anger subsided, I met with his side profile. Like the rest of him, it was deliciously hot as well. "Totally different question. You can't say no to this one."

He rolled his eyes. I ignored him. He was only pretending to be bored, but in reality, he was enjoying our banter.

Like he always did, or at least he did a million years ago.

"Last night at the party, you told Professor Sinclair that I live close to her. How do you know where I live?"

This time Nick kept his eyes on the road, but I could practically see the wheels turning inside his head. "You remember last summer when Ryan went to Boston to see you?"

I nodded. Of course I remembered. I spent an entire day hanging out with Ryan. During our dinner, I introduced him to Mike, which pissed me off because Ryan didn't remember him. Although that was partly my fault because Mike and I weren't always into public displays of affection. Probably that's why Ryan assumed that whatever was between us wasn't serious and wouldn't last.

Sure, Mike and I didn't have much chemistry. Nor was I in love with him. But did every relationship have to be built on chemistry and love? Certainly not.

"I was there with him." Nick's response brought me back to now. "Ryan and I had a business meeting that morning near your building. He showed me where you live."

"You were in Boston? And you didn't make time to see me?"

Hearing this loudly, I wasn't even certain if I felt hurt, or sad, or both. Even if he wasn't interested in me as a woman, I never expected Nick to alienate me from his life completely.

I turned away from him and looked out the window, unsure if I wanted to know more.

But Nick kept going. "We've been thinking of buying a hotel in Boston. That's what the business deal was about. We went together so I could attend a few meetings while he spent time with you."

That didn't help either, but I didn't want to put him on the spot any more than I already had. I knew where I stood in Nick's life.

Correction: I always knew. Then why was I so surprised and hurt?

Because deep down, I want to be wrong. I want him to want me like I want him. Madly. Crazily. Completely.

"Ahem." He cleared his throat, bringing me out of my rumination. "Ivy?"

"Yeah?"

"Have you thought about me in all these years?"

Every night, in every dream… I went to sleep thinking about you and I woke up thinking of you. You took away my nightmares and filled them with beautiful dreams. Your eyes, your smile…you gave me company…you made me happy. I shared all my secrets with you, and you didn't even know it.

I didn't respond. Instead, I thought of Boston and Mike, and how the two of them combined kept me grounded and safe.

From extensive buildings to lush fields, and congested streets to wide open roads, the scenery started changing outside my window. Green pastures, giant maple trees, white barns every few miles—the beautiful countryside calmed my soul. Even with the cloudy sky that suited the melancholy in my heart, the view was nothing short of picturesque.

Another half hour went by before Nick exited the highway and turned onto a local road.

The road felt familiar. Nick took his time, and I knew why. The three bicyclists who zoomed past us didn't share the same sentiment. A few more followed, the bike tires turning so fast that I could barely see the spokes… and that took me back to another day out on a similar road with bikes… a day long before this one.

"Dad! Ivy is hurt. She's been bleeding badly!" Nick's panicked voice filtered through the sound of my own sobs. "Tom is bringing the car around. I'm taking her to the hospital. I know the blizzard is getting out of control, but I can't reach Ryan. They're probably way ahead of us. No, I didn't try anyone else."

The blizzard prediction had been in the news, but the day had started off with clear sunny skies. No one had expected a complete whiteout in a matter of a few hours.

The desolate road stretched endlessly before us, devoid of any signs of life. The barren landscape offered no solace, not even a chirping of a bird or a scuttle of an insect nearby. We found refuge against the jagged rocks. Beyond those cold stones was death and Nick had saved me from it. Two damaged bikes lay on the side. Unrecoverable. Abandoned.

"Maybe I'm bleeding, too. I don't know," Nick said. With my head pressed against his chest, I could only hear one side of the conversation. "I don't care, Dad. I need to get Ivy to safety before this snow makes it impossible to reach the hospital."

My head turned to access his hand, which was squeezing me tightly against him. I was bleeding, but he was oozing blood. We both wore white sweaters, and they were covered in blood.

I tried lifting his sweater to look at his wound, but he instructed me not to move. His sweater had ripped. That was as much as I could see. My fingers were freezing, even though I was wearing my gloves, and I could hardly feel my feet in the frigid air.

A black SUV screeched to an abrupt halt, sending wet, black mud and snow flying into the air. Tom, Nick's driver, jumped out of the car to open the door for us. Nick scooped me up in his arms and carefully put me in the back seat, and then got in and took me on his lap.

"Nick, you're hurt," I managed. He was bleeding a lot. I realized that all the blood on our sweaters was his because I was only bleeding from my ankle. Seeing how much blood he had lost, I started crying again.

"I'm so sorry, Ivy. Taking this route was a terrible idea. I should've known better. What the hell was I thinking?" He pulled me into his chest again. "Please don't cry. I can't see you in pain. I am so, so sorry."

Nick wrapped his arms around me, covering me in his warmth. I couldn't tell him I wasn't crying because I was in pain. The only pain I cared about was his.

Snuggling into the crook of his neck, I suddenly felt at home.

"I didn't realize there was a cross-country bike race going on today." His voice pulled me out of our shared memory. "I can't believe they still haven't fixed these roads."

When I didn't respond for some time, he said, "I answered all of your questions, Ivy. Can I expect you to answer some of mine?"

I rubbed my throat, hoping the lump of pain would subside. I didn't know if he truly wanted an answer to his question or if he needed a distraction to take his mind off of the stalling cars.

"Last night you asked me why I'm fighting you. But the thing is, there is nothing to fight against. I remember how you treated me before I left for Boston. I remember you coming home with Celine."

"Celine? Out of everything we shared, she's who you remember?" His face contorted, turning a shade of red.

I glared at him. *Was he seriously mad at me?* "Exactly." My voice filled with indignation that matched his mood. "You knew I liked you and you threw Celine in my face. I remember you never coming after me. I remember you never attempting to contact me. And I remember you going after every woman in the freaking world instead of giving me a chance."

"Ivy, I—"

"Please stop." As blinded as I was by all the old hurt, I needed to concentrate on my present and my future. "I have a boyfriend now and unlike you, he is kind and caring. You are Ryan's friend. That's where our relationship begins and ends."

Chapter 7

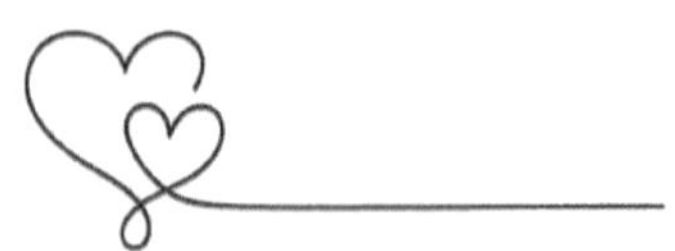

Half an hour later, we turned onto a gated private road with brass lion statues on either side of it. Plush, perfectly manicured grass, colorful flower beds, and old chestnut trees lined both sides of the road. It was another mile or so before the long road ended in a huge circular driveway with a tiered fountain in the middle.

We stopped in front of a breathtakingly gorgeous all-white estate. Unless I suffered from amnesia and didn't know it, I had never been here in my life.

My confusion was apparent. Nick said, "Welcome home. Mom and Dad are looking forward to meeting you."

I paled.

I hadn't seen them in years. Rosanne had called me after the last holiday I was at their house, but I didn't pick up the phone. After many more days of trying to reach me, she stopped calling altogether. I never called her or Xavier, either.

With trepidation in my heart, I walked toward the house. The briny embrace of the ocean air enveloped me and tried to calm my nerves.

That dreadful Christmas Eve night danced in front of my eyes. My shattered dreams of ever being Nick's. The pain of seeing Nick with another woman. I couldn't bear my incomplete life. A life without him. The wounds from the accident the year before were long healed. Rosanne didn't let me leave her home until I was back on my feet. Who would've thought that that would be the last good time I would have with this family... My extended family.

No proper goodbye; just a note on the kitchen counter saying that I had to leave to finish some urgent school assignment. Everybody knew it was a bullshit excuse, but who would question me? The only people who had the authority to call me out for being rude and ungrateful had left the world a long time back.

My parents' deaths had changed me completely. After the Celine incident, I broke ties with the last link to my past as well. I avoided people and hid further in my books. The only person I spoke to was Ryan.

That routine continued until I went to college and met my roommate, Abby. She forced me to hang out with her every weekend. We went on double dates—most of which I didn't enjoy—and after every heartbreak; I was always there to help her heal. She started bringing me to her house for the holidays.

It was at one of Abby's holiday parties, around two years ago, that Mike and I met.

Rosanne and Xavier were nothing but good to me—true parental figures that I needed in my life. And yet I had left their home in a huff, essentially replaced them, and refused to stay in touch.

Ryan called me the next morning, multiple times. I texted him back after I reached Boston, saying that I had forgotten about an assignment I had to submit. He had to have known it was a lame excuse, but he had not pushed me any further.

Nick joined me on the front porch. "This is our ancestral home," he explained. "Mom and Dad moved to Greenwich three years ago. You would've known had you stayed in touch."

Before I could defend myself and my choices, I heard my name and saw Rosanne coming to the foyer. Next to me, Nick's phone rang. He removed the phone from his jeans pocket and walked toward the garden with distress. "Make it quick," was all I heard.

"Oh, Ivy, dear! There you are!" Rosanne came closer and embraced me in a warm hug.

When I hugged her back, it felt like old times again. She reminded me of my mother in more ways than one.

And you chose to avoid her all these years.

"Let me look at you, my beautiful girl. Where have you been hiding all this time?" Her warmth reached her vibrant green eyes, and she pulled me back into another hug.

Only after she released me did I notice the tears. "You have such a striking resemblance to Sandra. Beautiful. A breath of fresh air."

She kept looking as if trying to find her lost friend in my face. I had some features from my mom, but I mostly looked like my dad.

Xavier joined us shortly. He pulled me into a hug and kissed me on both cheeks. "Set aside some time for us old folks, will you? We've some serious catching up to do."

Apprehension gave way to warmth, and my heart filled with love. It felt as if we were simply picking up where we left off, chatting away as if we had just spent a weekend apart.

"I love the way you have decorated this house, Rosanne. Even with its massive structure, it still feels like a home. Reminds me a lot of how Mom had decorated our penthouse in the city."

"That's because we both studied architecture and had a passion for interior design. Our styles were so similar that at one point, our professors thought Sandra and I were working on every project together." Rosanne chuckled, recalling the memory.

She gave me another hug like she genuinely missed me. "I want you to come back for the holidays again. We miss seeing you, dear."

"I miss you and Xavier, too. I'll be better about visiting more often, I promise. But only if you give me a tour of your rose garden today. I noticed it as we were pulling in. It's stunning."

Her face lit up. Our love for roses had blossomed over several years.

"Whenever you got together, you couldn't stop talking. I guess some things never change."

We both turned to the sound of Nick's voice. He stood in the doorway, watching us intently.

"Well, at least someone appreciates the work I have put into this house. When I die, I'm leaving it to Ivy, Nicholas. You're not getting so much as a room in this property," Rosanne said, playfully admonishing Nick.

"I love you too, Mom." He kissed Rosanne on the forehead before embracing her in a hug.

"Sure, sure." She wasn't ready to give it a rest.

I was used to their love-hate relationship. Behind her hard exterior, Rosanne was a softie for her only son and, as she had shown Ryan and me more than once, anyone else who needed love and support, too.

"How about this," I intervened. "When I buy my house, I would like you to decorate it for me."

"You've got yourself a deal, Missy. I look forward to that day."

Getting out of Nick's embrace, Rosanne called us over into a formal dining room. I followed her while Nick took the other door. "Are you expecting many people?" I asked Rosanne, counting the number of plates. There were over four.

"Not a lot. Just a few very important people. Lunch will be ready soon. Hope you brought your appetites with you!!"

"I'm famished, actually."

Even with all the grandeur and riches, the house had a warmth and coziness to it. Mom would've loved what Rosanne had done with the place.

"Ivy, dear. Can you come here for a minute?"

"Yeah, sure. On my way."

I ventured from room to room, trying to locate where Rosanne had gone—stopping as soon as I reached the den, because Taber was standing there beside the couch. He wasn't alone.

Ryan stood beside a strikingly beautiful woman I had never seen before. Smooth unblemished skin, captivating dark eyes, and lustrous waves of dark hair; her graceful poise effortlessly drew my attention. I had to force myself to look away from her and at my brother again.

A massive smile was plastered on his face and I could immediately tell he wasn't his usual self. Ryan didn't smile that way for no reason.

My first reaction was anger. I came to New York for him and he had seemingly forgotten that he had a sister at all. Still, I played it cool. The last thing I wanted was to throw a tantrum in front of these people.

"Happy to see you, big brother."

Shit, that came out way more sarcastic than I intended.

"Okay. I deserve that for ditching you last night," he admitted. "Before I beg for your forgiveness and try to make it up to you, I have some news to share."

At this point, I was done with surprises. But we weren't the only ones in the room, so I crossed my arms in front of me and braced myself for what was about to come. Besides, it was hard to be mad at Ryan when he looked this happy.

"Ivy," he said, taking the woman's hand and walking her toward me, "I want you to meet Risha. My fiancée."

Chapter 8

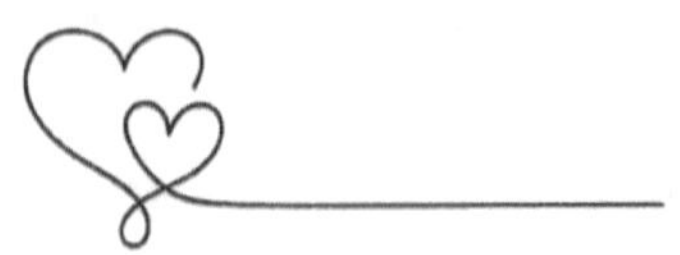

My poker face must've been flimsy at best, because Ryan took in my shocked expression and started laughing. The rest of the room erupted in cheers.

"We've been seeing each other for a few months now," Ryan explained, his grin getting wider by the second. "The more time I spent with her, the more right it felt. So last evening, I left the party early to propose to her and she said yes."

With a twinkle in my eyes, I turned to get a better look at Risha. She had a warm smile, stunning light olive skin, high cheekbones, and a delicate nose. She was breathtaking, as was the ring that glimmered on her finger—my mother's ring, which spoke volumes. If he had given that to Risha, that could mean only one thing: This was as serious as it could be. She was *the one*.

Never in my wildest dreams did I imagine my workaholic brother in a relationship, much less engaged. Yet here he was, the happiest I had seen him in years.

Hot tears spilled down my cheeks, tears of adoration and delight. My brother was in seventh heaven. With everyone watching me, I couldn't find words that would sufficiently express how happy I was for him, so I did the only thing that felt right at the moment. I hugged them both.

"Oh my god, you're engaged!" I finally said. "But why the secrecy? Why didn't you tell me sooner?"

"I wasn't sure if Risha was going to say yes."

I raised my brows.

"That's why I didn't tell you anything yesterday," Ryan said. "And after she said yes, I wanted to be the first person to tell you. Hence the elaborate rigmarole to get you here."

"I'm first generation Indian-American. I'll be the first to break tradition and marry someone who's not from India," Risha explained, before turning to Ryan. "But you know how I feel about you. Saying no was out of the question."

Holy hell! Was Ryan…blushing?

"I'm so happy for you both. Truly." Dabbing the corners of my eyes, I turned to Risha. "Welcome to the family." This was not something I saw coming, but Nick was right. It was hands-down the best surprise of my life.

"Seems like we have a lot of catching up to do," I told the newly engaged couple once most of the others had dispersed.

"And that, my darling Ivy, is why I planned this last-minute gathering." Rosanne spoke from the other side of the room. "We all have so much to celebrate."

"Thank you for doing all of this, Rosanne. It means a lot." I dashed to her and hugged her like I would have hugged my mother if she were here.

Xavier popped his head in through the doorway. "More reasons to come back home?"

"I love you all so much," I said, feeling emotional all over again. "But I don't think I belong in New York anymore. I'm happy in Boston."

The energy in the room shifted right before my eyes.

As though wanting to break the tension, Rosanne called out, "Lunch will be ready shortly. Let's head to the dining hall."

As we settled down in an airy dining room, the servers brought in the most decadent dishes and filled everyone's champagne flutes. Our lunch today was slow braised pork cheek and seafood risotto. The house was buzzing with people, although I counted more servers than guests. Rosanne and Xavier had made sure no expense was spared to celebrate Ryan and Risha, and I loved them for it.

"Before we dig in, let's decide what everyone wants to do after lunch. I'm proposing a beach day." Everyone cheered at Rosanne's suggestion. "The clouds have cleared up and there's nothing better than getting a little sun on the beach."

"And at six, we're going to have a little gathering for Ryan and Risha's engagement," Xavier announced.

"That's right. Nothing big, I promise. It'll be family and close friends only," Rosanne quickly added.

"You really didn't have to do all this," Ryan said. Smiling and blushing… I couldn't… with my brother.

"What rubbish, Ryan! Would you have said the same thing to Sandra and Donald? Besides, Xavier and I love throwing parties no matter what the occasion. We old people need something to celebrate, especially when it comes to celebrating the people we love. Getting to boogie and drink is nice, too."

We all laughed in unison. Branson parties had been the talk of the town as far back as I could remember.

"When did you find the time to plan? And who can come at such short notice?" Risha asked, sounding as surprised as I was.

"All the plans were put into motion as soon as you said yes," Xavier told her. "The people who are coming love Ryan dearly and they are excited to meet you. They didn't mind canceling their plans to be here tonight."

Once again, my eyes welled up. Not having mom and dad around left a huge dent in our lives. Learning to grow up without our parents wasn't easy, but knowing we still had people who cared about us and loved us as much as our parents had? That made their absence a little easier to bear.

As the chatter continued, I occasionally caught Nick watching me from the other side of the table. I suppose I was doing the same thing to him.

The kiss from last night was still burning in my mind and the butterflies in my stomach wouldn't rest. They didn't care that he still had the power to hurt me. Apparently, my heart and the rest of my body had minds of their own. Going against what was safe and right, they yearned for him.

I yearned for him. Badly.

To get my mind off the turmoil, I struck up a conversation with Risha since she was sitting next to me. "I love your earrings," I told her, eyeing the white and green butterflies. "They're really beautiful."

"Thank you. My younger sister made them," she mentioned proudly.

The way the earrings carried different hues of green, all blended with the white stones and gold accents, was remarkable. "So, your sister is an artist."

"It's more of a hobby for her. But if she wants to turn it into a career, I'm all for it. The busier she is making jewelry, the less time she has to get into mischief," Risha chuckled.

The more I learned about her sisters and how close they all were, the happier I was with the decision to come home—even if it was only for a week. I wouldn't have been part of this celebration had I stayed in Boston.

"I get it. We should all do what makes us happy and try to stay away from trouble as much as possible."

"Well said, Ivy." Xavier spoke from across the table. "What's next now that you're done with your undergrad?"

"I've already enrolled in the Harvard Business School's MBA program," I told him. "Not sure if I'll want to get another degree or do something else after that, so I'm taking it one step at a time."

"MBA is great. But why Harvard?" Xavier asked. "Columbia has one of the best business programs. And I heard that Professor Sinclair, one of the top-ranking professors in the country, accepted a position at Columbia."

"I know." My lips pursed. "I met her last night at MoxTo and she told me all about it. To be honest, I'm really disappointed."

"Do you want me to talk to the dean at Columbia?" Xavier asked. "You know I don't mind pulling a few strings for you."

"Thank you, but you don't have to do that. I wanted to be in Professor Sinclair's class and I'm definitely not happy about her switching universities, but I have no plans to leave Harvard or Boston."

Again, the mood in the room shifted. Suddenly, I felt like I was in the hot seat.

Why does it matter where I live or what I do, as long as I am happy?

"Give that poor child a break, Xavier. She is here with all of us today and that's good enough for me." Rosanne once again tried to break the tension.

With that, everyone returned to their own conversations—except for Xavier, who kept looking at me. I wasn't sure if what I saw in his eyes was sadness or pity.

Taber, sitting directly across from me, jumped to a new topic. "Please don't tell me you support the Red Sox now?"

Everyone found it hilarious, so I jested a little. "Of course I do. They are the best in the league," I said with a glint in my eye, knowing how much that would rile him up.

All the women in the house, along with Xavier, couldn't control their laughter while the boys looked at each other in complete disbelief.

"After all the Yankees games you dragged me to, rain or shine?" Ryan said indignantly. "Unbelievable."

I gave him a playful shrug. "What can I say? People change."

"And your favorite nightclub in Boston?" Taber had to ask. After all, he owned so many of them.

I made a disinterested face that unfortunately caught everyone's attention. Not that I didn't go to nightclubs, but that wasn't exactly my thing.

"You're right, Ivy." Rosanne was the one to pick on it and address it. "It's time to pack up your nightclub life and settle down, boys. Ryan is doing it. Let's see who follows."

To steer the conversation, Taber spoke again, "What did you say about the Red Sox, Ivy? In Connecticut, which is New York's sister state, you can't support the Red Sox. Like in New York, we don't support the New England Patriots."

He reminded everyone of my unwavering loyalty to the Patriots' team since I was a little kid. I couldn't help it. They were undoubtedly the best. And it had nothing to do with me living in Boston for the past eight years.

"I am sorry." I started picking at my food, trying to hide from this unwanted limelight. I had been caught off guard.

"Loosen up, Ivy. We don't actually care if you support the Patriots, Yankees, or the Red Sox. We're messing with you,"

Noticing me chewing on my bottom lip, Taber showed some mercy. "So, are you seeing anyone in Boston?"

"She doesn't believe in love," Ryan cut in. "She has a comfortable companion named Mike who she is planning to move in with for god-knows-what reason."

Irritated, I gave Ryan a sideways glance. What he just said was wrong on so many levels.

My eyes shifted to Nick, expecting him to gloat since he liked to make me uncomfortable and Ryan had given him the ammunition; but his face was practically expressionless.

"If you don't believe in love, look at your brother and Risha, Ivy. It does exist." Rosanne gave my shoulder a squeeze.

"When are you introducing us to Mike?" Xavier asked.

"Good question, Xavier. I'd love to meet this guy. What does he do?" Taber couldn't help but chime in.

I wasn't in a sharing mood, but figured I'd rather get it over with. "Mike is starting his doctoral program this fall. Now that my roommate is leaving for UCLA, Mike asked if we should move in together. I said yes."

"So, you guys will be roommates, then?" Nick asked.

My cheeks flushed. I hated being put on the spot, and I especially hated people picking apart my relationships.

"Give it a rest, Nicholas," Rosanne admonished him, once again coming to my rescue. "She won't want to come to anyone's engagement parties if we treat her this way. Unless the party is taking place at the Red Sox's Fenway stadium."

The room erupted in laughter. I nonchalantly shook my head. "Okay, okay. I can see what's happening here. Let's all bully the newbie."

"Technically, Risha is the newbie," Taber said. "But it's more fun to tease you."

The banter went on. I had to admit it; I was a little rusty at first. Clearly, I had stayed away from this family for far too long.

I got the hang of it and found my groove by the time lunch ended, though.

"We didn't have a chance to get to know each other yet. So how about we fix that?" Risha said once we got up from the table. "Mind if we head down to the beach and talk?"

"I'd love that! Let me change and I'll see you in a few."

Chapter 9

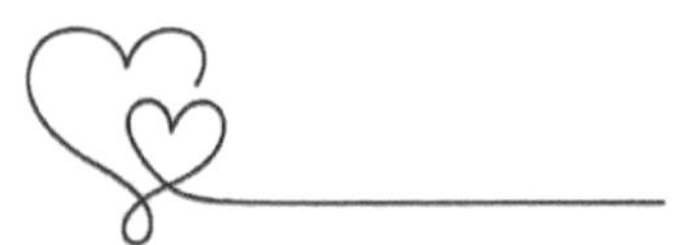

I entered the guest room, my duffle bag was already waiting for me. This room was different from the one in their Woodbury home. With plenty of pink and purple accents, Rosanne had set up that room for a teenage girl. Beautifully decorated in her signature style, she made sure I would find my home and my mother in that house.

And yet you ran away and never stayed in touch because you were mad at their son.

I swallowed down the regret and took in the room before me. This room was large. The walls displayed warm green tones that perfectly matched the green patchwork quilt draping the queen-sized bed. A large window overlooked the driveway below and let in a fair amount of sunlight. A full-length mirror with inbuilt lights was affixed to the wall.

Definitely a handy thing to have when it's time to get dressed for the evening.

Now, with a party to attend, a trip downtown was imminent.

No party dresses in my duffel bag, but I had packed a bathing suit for some reason.

Who knew that having a tendency to pack half of my life whenever I went anywhere could be a good thing?

Holding my swimsuit in one hand, I opened the door of the attached bathroom with another. As soon as I walked inside and locked the door, I felt *his* presence.

I turned and met with a set of gorgeous eyes. "Nick? What are you doing here?"

"Looks like we share a bathroom."

"Like hell we do. This can't possibly be your room."

"Ah, you see, this is my house. I can be in any bedroom I want and use any of the bathrooms I feel like."

He gave one of his heart-melting smiles. This man sure knew how to use his assets.

"Okay. Then I'm moving to another room." Desperate to get away from him before my body reacted to him the way it usually did, I turned and reached for the doorknob.

"Ivy, wait." He pressed his hand to the door. "We need to talk."

"About what?"

"I don't know," he mentioned casually. "How about you tell me about how much you love Mike."

"Ryan doesn't know shit. Don't take his words literally."

"So, he's wrong and you're both madly in love with each other?"

"Why do you care?"

"I want to know who I'm competing against."

"There is no competition, Nick."

"Good to know. It's clear you'd pick me over him."

With a long exhale from the depths of my belly, I confronted him. "I don't get you. I come back and suddenly you're interested in me? Actually, you know what? It doesn't matter whether you are or aren't. Tell me what you want and leave me be."

After a long, pregnant pause when he didn't respond, I turned back to the door.

"How can I ever explain myself if you keep on walking away?" He pulled me by my waist and soon I was back in his arms. Electricity crackled between us. I once again found myself weak and helpless next to him. "Does he make you feel like this?"

The more I struggled to push him away, the more he dragged me into him. The physical roughness, combined with an animalistic need, surprised me and aroused me to a point I had never felt.

"Let me go, Nick. You're too late." My empty effort to get out of his hold did nothing to change our situation.

The searing heat that emanated from his body tempted me. My senses were heightened as his chest pressed against my back. Resisting him was quickly becoming an uphill battle.

My skin flushed when I felt his hot breath on my ear. Adrenaline rushed through me and blood pumped through my veins. Every pore of my being started opening up for him.

"Do you react the same way when he is near you?" Nick whispered in my ear. This closeness affected him, too. Equally. The rise and fall of his chest gave it away.

"Stop this madness, Nick," I said between shallow breaths, unable to keep my desires in check.

"You're not the only one seeking answers here, Ivy. Are you drawn to him like you are to me?"

It took everything in my power not to turn and surrender to him, to stay upset with him instead...

Why was I upset with him again?

"Look at me, Ivy."

I wasn't ready to face him. I didn't want him to find out how I felt about him. He was late. He was *four years* late.

"Breathe." Nick's tongue caressed the rim of my ear.

A moan escaped my lips. Every part of my skin was hypersensitive to his touch. I was powerless against him. "Why are you doing this to me?" I asked, my words hardly audible even to my own ears.

"Accept it, Ivy. We are destined to be." Turning me around, his lips brushed against mine. Fire crackled between us.

He started with a slow, gentle kiss, testing me and teasing me; but soon he grew more demanding. With every stroke of his tongue, he challenged me to prove what a bad idea holding back was. His every lash asked me to join him, to be in this moment with him.

He explored me with his mouth, with his tongue, as if trying to understand me and show me how attracted he was to me.

It was taking a toll not to respond to his demands, not to give in.

I didn't join.

He didn't stop.

The kissing intensified. Nick was testing my limits, and I was feeling powerless. Moving his hands to my face, he tilted my head back and his tongue dipped further, deepening our intense kiss. He started exploring every inch of my mouth with that kiss, every ridge and every crevice. He wanted to possess me.

Holding myself back was impossible. I started giving in to his insistence. My fingers clenched his hair. I started kissing him back with a maddening passion that matched his. With my eyes closed and my senses heightened, I took my time touring his mouth.

My hands explored his hard biceps over his soft T-shirt. Now that he had unleashed the beast inside me, I wanted to touch every inch of him. I couldn't wait to see him naked. His closeness, his caresses—I had waited far too long for this.

He placed his hand on the back of my neck to hold me steady. My hand moved to chase him with my fingers. A deep, chesty groan escaped him.

We were so drunk with passion that by the time we realized that someone was knocking on my door, the knocking had become insistent and loud.

I pushed Nick away with all my might, the passion that we shared a moment ago fizzling out like it was never there.

Nick let out a frustrated growl. "We need to talk." And then he went back to his room, leaving me all alone.

Chapter 10

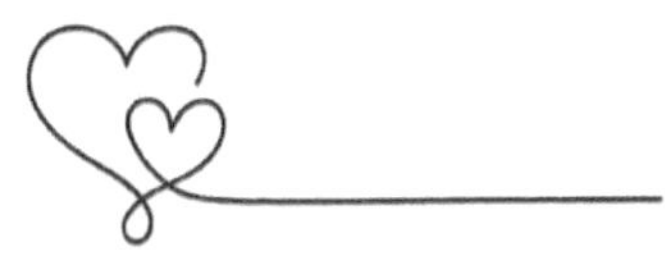

As soon as I made sure that Nick was nowhere to be seen and it was safe to exit the bathroom, I opened the door and met with a familiar face.

"Oh my gosh. Is that really you? It's been forever since I last saw you!" Cece, Taber's younger sister, smiled at me brightly. Her red lipstick made her perfect white teeth glow.

She looked the same, right out of my memory—long nose, blue eyes, sharp jawline—though somehow her golden locks had transformed into a short black bob. She was a total knockout. In an oversized button-down shirt and an orange miniskirt, she oozed confidence.

We embraced. She even wore the same perfume she used to wear back when we were teenagers.

"It's so good to see you. How come nobody told me you'd be coming?"

"It was kind of a last-minute thing," Cece explained. "I wasn't supposed to be here until later in the evening. Risha called me this morning and said you'd be here, so of course I had to come immediately."

I noticed a bag at her feet. She must've just arrived.

"I was about to head to my room, but then I asked the housekeeper where you were staying. When she told me, I came to say hi to you first," she said. "We have so much catching up to do!"

"We do. Did you bring a bathing suit? Everyone's heading down to the beach."

"I sure did. I'm going to run to my room and change. Meet you downstairs?"

"Sounds good."

I slipped back into the bathroom—only this time, to avoid surprises, I locked both doors before changing into my backless neon green swimsuit. It was leaning towards sexy, but as the hip kids said: *YOLO!* I checked the mirror and was happy with what I saw. Before I headed out, I grabbed a gold sarong out of my bag and wrapped it around my waist.

I could embrace the "you only live once" attitude, but that didn't mean I had to throw all modesty out the window.

By the time I went downstairs, Cece was nowhere to be seen. Outside, the backyard was buzzing with preparations for tonight's party.

People were running around with flower bouquets. A lady who was probably the party planner gave orders to her staff. This place was pure organized chaos.

Deciding to leave the commotion behind, I walked through a little gate and made my way to the private beach.

A full-blown picnic area had been set up with large beach umbrellas and lounge chairs. There were tables with all sorts of snacks and drinks. Ryan and Taber were in the middle of a beach volleyball game. Cece, looking stunning in her red polka-dot bikini, noticed me and waved. Rosanne and Risha were sunbathing and chitchatting, while Xavier was busy in the makeshift bar area, talking to the bartenders and servers they'd hired to take care of their guests.

After the encounter I'd had with Nick, naturally my first destination was the bar. I made my way over to Xavier.

Distinguished and quite the style icon, even at his age, Xavier must've turned heads when he was younger. From what my parents had told me, his life had taken a full one-eighty-degree turn when he met Rosanne because once he did, they only had eyes for each other.

Both of them came from money, but Rosanne must've had more of it because her family was worried that Xavier was only marrying her for her wealth. But Xavier only wanted Rosanne, and Rosanne wanted him. Once they got married, she ended up giving all the money she inherited to her brother. It could've been a dangerous move, but with Rosanne by his side Xavier took his family wealth to the next level and became a major Wall Street mogul.

And now Nick was taking the Branson business to a whole new level through asset diversification and investing in venture capital, with Blue Chip being one of the companies he invested in. I still hadn't gotten over the coincidence that he had bought that company around the same time that I started interning there.

"Should we celebrate your return with more champagne?" Xavier's voice brought me back to the present.

"Let's keep the toasting for the evening. I would love a beer, though" I said.

He motioned to the bartender, who placed five bottles on the counter. "Take your pick."

So I did, and the bartender opened it up for me.

Xavier looked down at my ankle, which was atrociously visible because of my flats. "Your scar is still noticeable. Does it ever hurt?"

"Not at all. Most of the time I don't even remember it's there," I lied.

"Ever thought of getting rid of it? I know a great specialist in the city who could do that."

"Never." I looked down at the unmistakable mark. The six-inch scar was a part of me I didn't want to change, as much as my brown hair that I got from my mother. "It's part of me now."

Xavier watched me intently. It seemed he was going to say something, but at the last minute, he changed his mind.

"How are you really doing, Ivy?" he asked after a brief pause. "I want to understand your fascination with Boston. It can't be the weather or the people."

"And definitely not the Red Sox," I quickly added with a chuckle.

He let out a hearty laugh. Although we didn't see eye-to-eye as far as Boston went, I loved his warmth and how much he cared about me. He had always taken a genuine interest in my time at Harvard. Even today, he listened intently as I told him about my MBA plans and explained that after living in Boston for so many years; it felt like home now.

"Reconsider Columbia, Ivy. You're going to love it there," Xavier tried, unabated. To put his mind at ease and to give myself time to process the misfortune that was Professor Sinclair leaving Harvard, I promised him I would.

Eventually, Rosanne joined us. "I hope he's not bothering you about Boston again, Ivy."

"No, we're all good here. I was telling Xavier how at home I feel in Boston."

"You went to school there, you have friends there—that's natural. When we left Manhattan it wasn't an easy change either, but now I can't even imagine going back to city life."

"It's all about what we get comfortable with. But just because we are comfortable doesn't necessarily mean it's the best choice for us. Sometimes we need to push our boundaries to see what else is out there," Xavier advised.

We all went quiet. Clearly, he was trying to tell me something… something I wasn't ready to hear.

"Enough of it, love. Ivy is an adult now and she can decide what's best for her."

I cut in before Xavier could respond. "It's been ages since I've gone swimming in the ocean. I'd love to take a dip, but first I should get sweaty and win a few points."

"Ready for some action, sis?" Ryan asked loudly, as he pushed the ball over the volleyball net.

"Finish this round and we'll see!" I shouted, so they could hear me over the sound of crashing waves.

Risha jogged over to where I was. "Let's show these boys what we've got!"

Although I had just met her, it was clear we would get along well.

It was also obvious this wasn't her first time meeting these people. A tinge envious, I couldn't stop myself from going back to the time when I was part of this family. These people had been my everything, and yet I ran away because I couldn't stand Nick being with someone else.

"I'm in for a game," Cece called out from her beach chair.

I left my half-finished beer on the table nearby and joined them. We played for the next forty-five minutes and though I wasn't the best at volleyball, I ended up earning a couple of points for my team.

After the game, Ryan, Risha, and I headed to the snacks table while the rest went for a swim.

"You were pretty good with the saves," Ryan said. "Almost like a pro. I was pretty impressed." As if I was a kid that needed praise.

"Just so you know, complimenting my athletic abilities won't get you out of trouble." I picked up a grape from the tray and tossed it in my mouth. "You had no right to bring up our private conversation at the lunch table." I knew I wouldn't be able to get it out of my system until we talked it out.

Ryan rubbed his palm against the back of his head. "By the time I realized my mistake, I had already said it and there was no going back. But you're right. I shouldn't have done it. I'm sorry." He made a sad face and added, "I promise I'll make it up to you."

"You better, because right now you're at the top of the list of people I will target if the Purge ever becomes a thing." I reminded him of the horror movie that we once watched together back at the Hampton house. We had both had nightmares for weeks.

"I hear you loud and clear." He nudged me with his shoulder. I nudged him right back to let him know we were back to being on good terms.

"Did you know that I have Cece to thank for this?" Risha announced enthusiastically, as she flashed me her engagement ring.

"You do? How?"

"We met at one of Cece's parties. Cece and I've known each other since our undergrad. Same college, same majors. We were roommates and best friends for years… and Ryan was Taber's close friend. Yet we never met until recently."

"Wow, what a small world." Disheartened to be out of the loop, I realized I knew little about the woman my brother was going to marry. "I love Cece. I don't know anyone who doesn't. Are you still living together?"

"Actually," Ryan joined in, glancing at Risha, "we moved in together a few months ago."

"Slowly all the secrets are coming out," I laughed, though deep down I was ashamed of knowing so little about my brother's life. "But if you live together, how come I didn't see you at the apartment yesterday?"

"Yesterday was a busy day for me. And after Ryan proposed, we ended up celebrating all night." The spark in Risha's eyes was undeniable.

While I was reliving my heated, ravenous kiss with Nick all night, they were celebrating their engagement.

"Sorry, Ivy," said Ryan. "A lot of planning went into this proposal and then we ended up moving up the hotel opening. It was only days ago you told me you'd be visiting, and by then there was no way for me to change any of the plans."

Now it made complete sense as to why Ryan was nowhere to be found all that evening.

"Please don't apologize," I told him. "Your proposal clearly went well because Risha said yes, and now we're all here together. That's all that matters."

Ryan wrapped his arms around Risha and pulled her closer. I was ecstatic to see my brother so madly in love. He had found his soulmate, someone who could help him forget the pain he endured. I couldn't be happier for him.

"Risha, you said that your family wasn't crazy about the idea of you marrying someone who's not Indian. Are they okay now?" I asked, remembering her comment from earlier this morning.

Risha chuckled. "I'm not giving them much of a choice, am I? My family is very important to me, but so is Ryan. We have some work ahead of us."

"That seems like *a lot* of work. Are you up for the challenge?"

"When you love someone, you can move mountains to make things work," Risha glanced at Ryan. Some unspoken understanding passed between them. "And he is worth all the challenges in the world."

Ryan gave her a peck on the lips. I wished mom and dad were here to see him this relaxed and, finally, at peace.

And what do they see when they look at you? How miserable is your own life since you have decided to never fall in love and chose a "safe" guy for the sake of protecting your heart?

"Nothing makes me happier than knowing how much my brother means to you." Keeping my thoughts at bay, I rejoined the conversation. "Are there any more surprises I should know about before I go for a dip?"

Ryan chuckled and got right to the point. "Actually, there is one more thing."

I couldn't. What's with Ryan and surprises?

"We are thinking of heading to the Caribbean Islands to celebrate our engagement, but only if it's okay with you. Otherwise, we can move the trip to some other time."

"Absolutely not. You both deserve some time away and the Caribbean sounds like the perfect place. Don't even think about changing your plans for my sake. Besides, I have plans to catch up with my school friends and visit some of my old hangout places. You don't have to worry about me."

I lied again because I was here for him. Seeing him so happy, I wouldn't do it any other way.

"In that case, we'll stick with our original plan and fly out tomorrow morning. Xavier is lending us his private jet."

"Fancy," I noted. "That sounds like so much fun."

Ryan put his arm around my shoulders as we headed toward the ocean, something he had been doing since we were little. "You've really grown up, Ivy. Thank you for being so supportive."

"Of course." Feeling like I needed to say it, I added, "I'm always here for you two."

Chapter 11

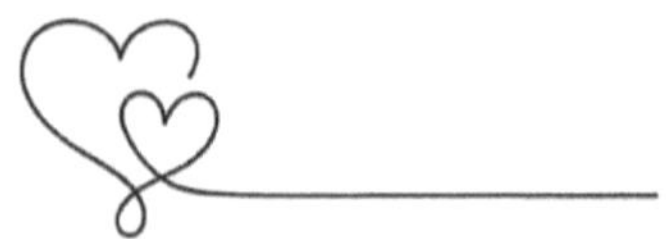

I stared at Nick's perfection, watching his calves flexing when he ran on the sand and his biceps bulging every time he tried to catch the ball. It had been ages since I last saw him without a shirt on. Once again, I couldn't take my eyes off of him.

Tall. Lean. Washboard abs. A light shadow of golden hair running down his torso and disappearing into his ocean blue swim trunks. With a taut jawline and a sharp nose—features hardened by time—he looked almost regal, and more attractive than ever before.

He jumped up to catch the ball, twisting in mid-air. It was a move he did with such perfection that I assumed he had practiced it for years. It also gave me a full view of the deep tissue scar that started at his shoulder and ended halfway to his elbow.

My bike's suspension broke when I rode over multiple jagged rocks all those years ago. The biting cold and the sudden whiteout made it impossible to see the road and before I knew it, my ankle caught in the wheel. Without caring for his safety, and trying to save me from sliding down the hill, Nick jumped off of his bike to grab me and landed right on the jagged rocks. Even through layers of clothing, it still sliced his arm.

And now, because of me, there was a scar on his otherwise perfect body.

I had wanted a ride on his Ducati, but Nick said no and wouldn't budge. Just to show how tough I was, I convinced everyone to go mountain biking instead.

If only I hadn't insisted so hard. Or pushed them to take the most challenging route. If only I had listened to Xavier and played pool in the basement instead. If only…

"There are five car accidents on the highway. Your family is stuck in the traffic jam of the decade. With the storm picking up, it will be a while before they get here."

I could hear the voice. It was the ER nurse talking to me as I started to come out of what felt like the deepest sleep of my life.

"Where is Nick? Nicholas… Can I see him?" My voice was hoarse and groggy. I could feel a numbing pain in my entire left foot.

"It took a great deal of convincing, but he finally agreed to be examined. The doctor is stitching him up as we speak. Speaking of which, your ankle —"

"How bad are his injuries? He was bleeding so much." Forgetting my discomfort and pain, I panicked. Tears streamed down my face. Both his white sweater and mine were completely red the last time I saw him. And it was entirely his blood.

"You need to stay calm. He is okay but he has lost a lot of blood. Once he gets stitched up, we might have to give him a blood transfusion. In case you're curious, your surgery was a success."

She put her hand on mine, trying to calm me down. It didn't help. Nothing was going to help until I could see him.

"How are you two related?" the nurse asked.

"He's my brother's best friend."

"Are you sure that's all he is to you? He didn't let any of the nurses even look at his wounds until the doctor confirmed that you were okay. You're lucky to have such caring people in your life."

Our eyes met.

He winked.

The salty breeze kissed my skin, the seagulls danced in the sky, and the blue ocean turned emerald green. The sand beneath my toes shifted. I locked eyes with him again, feeling a surge of electricity and the infinite possibilities. He took a step towards me.

My heart fluttered so fast that I lost my balance to the wave that came crashing into me. I sat up on my ass with a big grin. With a laugh, he shrugged halfway before returning to his game.

I got up on my feet and looked around to make sure no one saw us. Thankfully, everybody was too busy enjoying the beautiful weather to pay any attention to us.

I exhaled. Desperate to put some distance between me and Nick, what was I thinking? I joined Cece and Risha frolicking in the water.

After swimming for a good hour, we were back at the beach chairs to catch some sun rays. The evening's party discussion had started when it finally dawned on me. "Girls, it's my brother's engagement party and I have nothing to wear!"

"No biggie. We'll go shopping and find you something fabulous," Cece said with so much confidence that I believed her.

Risha told us they had an appointment with the stylist, wished us luck, and joined Ryan. Cece and I headed back to the house. As we rounded the volleyball net, Nick almost fell on top of us trying to catch the ball.

"Where are you girls heading?" he asked.

"Ivy needs a dress for the evening. I'm going to help her find one," Cece told Nick and with full determination, she headed back towards the house. I was on her tail.

Nick looked at his wristwatch. "It's almost three. Don't you think it's too late to go shopping?" Even his perplexed look couldn't put a dent in his perfect face.

Get a grip, Ivy.

"Party is not until six. Plenty of time to shop, grab a coffee, and get ready before the guests arrive."

Precisely why I freaking loved Cece. She could be up for anything, even though I agreed with Nick that we were on a time crunch.

He muttered something under his breath and threw the ball to Taber. "Fine. I'll take you, but you'll have to be done in one hour."

Cece looked at me. We were both thinking the same thing. "Two," we said in unison.

Nick smiled and kept the negotiations going. "One and a half."

"Done." I added, "Just so we're clear, that doesn't include getting there and driving back."

He rolled his eyes. "Fine. But I want to see you both in my car in fifteen minutes."

Determined to get away from him before he changed his mind, we ran toward the house.

I jumped into the shower to wash the salt water off of my skin, and then put on a white tank top and faded jeans. With no time to dry my hair, I left it down once again and slipped my feet into my favorite white ankle-high sneakers. By the time I was ready to go, Cece had already put on a gray jumpsuit and was waiting for me in the hallway.

Nick pulled out a black Range Rover from the underground garage. Cece got into the back and stretched out across the entire seat.

"Do you mind if I put my legs up?" she asked. "They're killing me. That's what I get for never going to the gym and then deciding to play volleyball and swim all on the same day."

"Sure, no problem." I opened the front door and sat with Nick.

These situations weren't exactly helping me maintain my distance from Nick. Any close contact, even by accident, was not good for my sensibility. The surrounding air was always charged with a powerful sexual undercurrent and I was tired of reminding myself to breathe every time he came near me.

"Ivy! Now that we've reconnected, promise me you'll stay in touch!" Cece got all chatty as she got comfortable.

"I promise I won't vanish this time."

"Taber said that you're moving to Boston. Is that right, Cece?" Nick asked.

"You heard right. I'm joining a new company. Their headquarters are in Boston, but once I get up to speed with the projects my plan is to transfer to their San Francisco office. Better weather there," Cece explained.

"My roommate is also moving to California, but she's heading to UCLA," I chimed in.

"Good for her! Maybe all three of us can do a road trip up and down the coast."

"Now that sounds tempting."

Cece turned to Nick. "So, Nick. How is Mindy doing? I guess we'll be meeting her this evening?"

"You know Mindy?" I spoke before I could stop myself. The intensity of my jealousy almost made my heart burst.

"Of course, I know her. Nick and Mindy have been the talk of the town for a while now."

I was ready to puke.

"That's a lie. Where are you getting all of this information from?" Nick's irritation seeped through his impatient tone.

"I get all my updates from Page Six, of course. *One of the most eligible bachelors in America has found his better half after all,*" she added with a dramatic flair, as if she were reading a gossip column. "I have to agree. You look great together."

"Sorry to disappoint, but none of this is true." He stubbornly refused to agree with Cece. She wasn't ready to accept that a gossip mag could lie.

For the rest of the ride they kept going back and forth about the legitimacy of the stories the papers ran, but I was barely listening. My brain was too busy processing facts. What I saw at MoxTo was very much real. However much Nick tried to pretend there was nothing between him and Mindy, Cece had just confirmed what I already knew.

Mindy and Nick were together. He had lied to me when he said they weren't.

If they were being photographed frequently, they were clearly seeing each other. Did Nick really think I would never find out? Or was he just hoping to have some fun on the side with me before he went back to his Mindy?

The thought sickened me to my core. Coming back home was turning out to be a huge mistake.

Don't forget who you're really here for, Ivy.

Ryan and Nick have been stuck at the hip since they were teenagers. How did I expect not to run into Nick?

We pulled up in the parking lot and Cece got out. She waved at me with her phone and answered a call.

Nick started speaking to me, but I couldn't hear a word. The blood pumping in my ears was the only sound I was aware of. All

I wanted right now was to get as far away from this man as possible.

I unfastened my seatbelt. Nick put his hand over mine, stopping me. "Talk to me," he said.

I couldn't.

He didn't move his hand away. "I didn't lie to you."

More lies.

I forced myself to look at him. I didn't want to be that weak, lovesick person anymore; but right at this moment, I was. And I hated myself for it.

"At least give me a chance to explain."

But there was nothing to explain here. He had a life of his own and so did I. We were different people in different phases of life.

I gathered all of my strength and pushed his hand away. "I have no right to be upset. You don't owe me an explanation. I've no intention of wasting my shopping time sitting in this car."

With that, I opened the door and got out.

Chapter 12

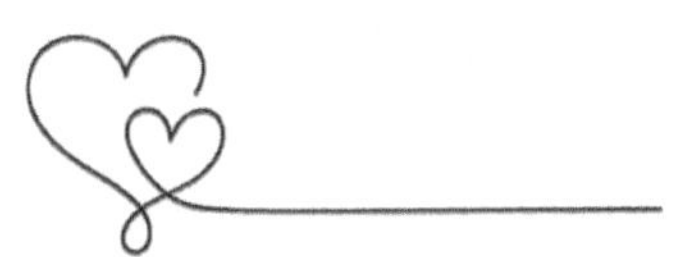

I lost interest in shopping, but I browsed the boutiques Cece hauled me to and faked excitement over the glittery things she dangled in front of me. It was Cece who picked my cocktail dress for the evening, stating how perfect it was for the occasion. The dress was too edgy for my taste, but it was easier to say yes than argue and prolong this shopping excursion.

After securing the outfits, we entered a nearby cafe, ordered coffee, and waited for Nick. Outwardly, I pretended to be calm and collected. I was an expert in hiding my feelings. But my insides were in knots and I wasn't looking forward to having him around. All I needed was my personal space, where no one could disturb me for days while I cried like a fool.

Again.

Cece talked so much that there wasn't any room left for awkward silence. She waved out the window when I saw Nick approaching the cafe. I didn't know what to make of everything between us, but I was sure of one thing: I hated the way my heart flipped every time I saw him.

He has a girlfriend, for the millionth time. The endless internal quarrels were pushing me to insanity.

Nick walked in and sat next to me. "We finished with time to spare. Are you proud of us?" Cece teased. I, on the other hand, had no intention of joining the conversation.

A phone started ringing. It wasn't mine. Cece dug into her oversized handbag and after the phone went on ringing for what seemed like a full minute, she finally got it out and hand-gestured *for ten minutes.*

Since I had no interest in sitting with Nick, I picked up my purse and stepped away.

In the unisex washroom line, I stood behind the man ahead of me. With nothing else to look at in the harshly lit white corridor, I checked my phone. Two missed calls from Mike. *Crap!* My phone was still on vibrate.

Ignoring it for now, I sent a quick message to Abby.

Miss you. Wish I was in Boston.

"Who was that for?"

I didn't bother to turn around. I could recognize Nick's voice even in my unconscious. Plus, I was always either aroused or irritated in his presence, so not meeting his eyes might've been a better bet.

Ignoring him, I waited for my turn. A woman stepped out. The guy ahead of me went inside and locked the door. My subconscious reminded me that Nick and I were alone in the corridor. It also reminded me that without high heels, I was almost a head shorter than him.

"You can't ignore me forever, Ivy," Nick said, his breath tickling the back of my head. I knew it wasn't intentional. I had a different reaction around him. When I didn't respond, he added, "I promise to keep my hands to myself. I just want to talk."

But his words and his actions didn't match. He was standing so close I could practically feel the heat of his body searing into mine, his masculine scent filling up my nostrils. The magnetic pull between us was too strong to ignore, and once again, I was having a hard time not leaning into him and giving in.

I couldn't blame him. Our physical attraction was palpable. But this was precisely our problem; after all these years of being apart, nothing had changed. Chemistry aside, we hadn't taken a single step forward.

"I don't want to talk to you. Leave me alone."

"That's not an option. Pick a time and a place."

I didn't turn around or look back. I said, "Our time has already passed. You should've sought me out years ago instead of waiting for me to pop up in your field of vision."

The atmosphere shifted when Nick moved and stood beside me. "Tell me what I have to do to change your mind."

I was tired of this internal battle and Nick wasn't making things any easier. "Don't you get it? I want nothing to do with you."

"Come on, Ivy. Be realistic. Are you seriously planning to lie to yourself for the rest of your life?"

Dizzy from his closeness and drawn to his voice, I was having difficulty keeping my desires in check.

When I didn't respond, he said, "Listen. We both had our own lives until yesterday, but that doesn't mean we can't sort out our problems and be together now."

I braced myself and turned to meet his eyes. "You, Nick. You are my problem. Other than that, my life is perfectly fine. Also, my life has absolutely nothing to do with yours. And I would like to keep it this way."

Right at that moment, the guy ahead of me came out of the washroom. I walked in and locked the door.

Once alone, I took a deep breath and tried not to overthink Nick's intentions. Surely, this was all just a game to him.

———————————————

Fifteen minutes later, I found Cece and Nick standing at the entrance and waiting for me. Once we reached the car and Nick started putting our shopping bags in the trunk, I took the opportunity to slip into the back seat.

I had no idea why I was hurting so much. It was impossible to think of Nick with another woman. This unbearable, unexplainable jealousy ate at me. When I tried imagining Mike with someone else, it didn't affect me one bit. So why did I feel so different about Nick?

Because you love him.

I was starting to hate this little inner voice that kept telling me ridiculous things. I didn't even know Nick.

Except that you do.

Hot, rich, and the sole heir of Branson Capital, Nick had always been the talk of the town. Getting interviewed for newspapers and having his pictures plastered all over them must've been second nature to him by now.

I had consciously stayed away from it all. The last thing I wanted to know was who he was dating or sleeping around with. The jealousy that consumed me when I first saw him with Celine left me miserable enough, but I'd had no choice because she appeared in his house with no warning. Since I didn't want that same pain inflicted upon me, I protected myself by ignoring everything and anything that had to do with Nick.

Mike was different. He was simple, loyal, and considerate. Life with him was uncomplicated. We had similar interests. He did whatever made me happy and gave me space whenever I needed it. He was right for me in every way.

And, yet, you can't commit to him. You keep him at bay on purpose. You don't even love him, Ivy. Wake up.

Cece and Nick chatted throughout the drive. I had no interest in listening or taking part. Covering my eyes with my big black shades, I hid the turmoil that was going on inside of me. The realization sat heavy in my chest—no matter how many years went by, I would never get over Nick Branson.

Chapter 13

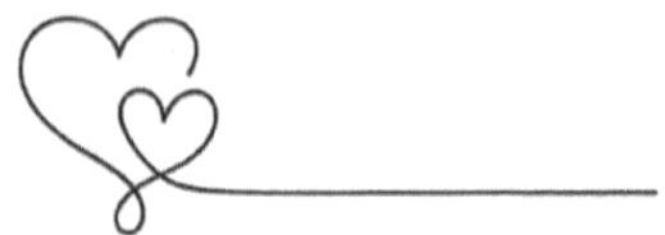

After a leisurely shower, I pulled my hair into a high bun and used my day-old makeup kit—nothing crazy, just foundation, and a red lip to match the sexiness of the dress. I slipped into my new cocktail dress that hit me mid-thigh—a dress which was nothing more than an oversized black blazer with heavy white and gold pearls scattered all over the fabric. The open V reached my navel. I put on a pair of black Louboutin booties, as well as a pair of chunky gold and pearl earrings that Cece had picked out for me at the same boutique.

In a gold halter neck dress, crimson sandals, and makeup with gold accents, Cece had outdone herself. One word—gorgeous!

"Let's have a drink before everyone else shows up," Cece said, after we had finished admiring each other's outfits and were heading downstairs.

A full bar with a bartender on duty stood between the kitchen and the formal dining area. I asked for a cosmo—my drink of choice since I left Boston—and inspected my reflection in the mirror next to the bar.

"This dress is too revealing," I whined, trying to adjust the front to cover whatever I could.

"Stop complaining. Thank God I went shopping with you, or you would've picked something plain and boring."

"That's not true." I immediately turned defensive. "What's wrong with the way I dress?"

"Boring. Your MoxTo's party ware on the gossip sites screamed 'boring.' You looked gorgeous but the dress didn't do you justice," Cece insisted.

I immediately decided on defending my choice. "You're blind. It has volume. Tight bodice. The color suited me. It was perfect."

"Like I said, boring." I couldn't take her boring song anymore, but she went on. "Today you're a bombshell. This dress is so *you*. Trust me on this."

And then I remembered last night. My belly trembled. Butterflies flew high.

Accept it, Ivy. You want Nick, and that feeling will not go away because you want it to.

Cece was still watching me intently. I blushed and tried to change the subject. "Seriously? One day in the city and there's already a picture of me in the gossip news? Ryan was so confident when he said the pictures wouldn't see the light of the day."

"Unfortunately, my dear, that's what the city does. If you hang out with these men, you're bound to be in the news."

"So how come you're not in the news? Unless you are and I don't know?"

She laughed at my ignorance. "Dad makes sure I never make it into any of these gossip columns. Also, I stay out of drama."

"Stay out of drama, got it," I said. "But see, that was one dress. You can't judge my sense of style on a single dress alone," I insisted. Not ready to let it go. I still believed the dress was gorgeous.

She raised a perfectly plucked eyebrow. "I need to see you more often to change my mind."

"You'll see me every day until you change your mind. I take fashion seriously."

Cece laughed, making me join her.

The clicking sound of high heels on the stairs interrupted our girl time. Rosanne came into view, with Xavier right behind her. Wearing a peach gown and dripping in diamonds, Rosanne still turned heads; but her vibrant green eyes, kind heart, and gentle smile were by far her best accessories.

She was a pixie compared to her husband, Xavier. But people could see that she had a hold on his heart like no one else. They were a made-for-each-other kind of couple.

Xavier walked over to the bar. His sandy brown hair, square jaw, and all-white tuxedo made him look dashing and a good decade younger than his actual age.

Nick had inherited his mother's eyes, but the rugged good looks he got from his dad. He had undoubtedly won the genetic lottery.

He is a sex god walking this earth and you want to worship his body.

"You girls look marvelous tonight." Rosanne hugged me and Cece and air-kissed us both.

"You and Xavier look wonderful too." Cece added her own compliment to those the amazing couple had already received.

"You really do." I joined the wagon. "By the way, did I tell you how much I love you both and how thankful I am that you're throwing this party in Ryan and Risha's honor?"

"I'm pretty sure you did, but I'll never not love hearing it."

We stood in a little circle and praised each other's dresses while Xavier got his drink.

Rosanne touched my arm. "Would you like to come to the entrance and greet the guests with us? They are all dear to Ryan.

You don't have to if you're not up for it, though," she added immediately.

I guess everybody knew about my antisocial tendencies.

"I would love to," I told her. After all, the guests were coming to celebrate my brother's engagement. What kind of sister would not greet them?

Hoping that the alcohol would help me get through all the schmoozing I would have to do, I gulped down the rest of my drink and started walking toward the entrance with Rosanne. Xavier was a few steps behind us, fixing his bowtie.

"Dressing up for parties suits you, Ivy, but it's your smile that makes you even more beautiful. It's identical to Sandra's." Rosanne's voice cracked slightly. "I can't tell you how happy we all are to have you here tonight."

"Thank you. I wouldn't have missed this for the world."

"We wouldn't have let you miss it, either. If you hadn't come today, we would've sent our charter to pick you up from anywhere in the world."

My big grin matched Rosanne's. I loved her so much that it hurt. Yet, I did what I did because I was crazy about her son.

"Ivy, Ryan misses you."

With those words, Rosanne knocked the air out of my lungs. My smile faded away.

"I know it's easy for siblings to grow apart because something similar happened to me and my brother," she went on. "The difference is that Ryan wants you in his life. He is trying. You should put in some effort as well."

"Rosanne, I—"

"I won't do what Xavier has been doing and ask you to come back. Do what makes you happy. Stay where you find peace, but don't run away from your roots. I'm pretty sure that's what Sandra would've wanted," she reminded me. "You're both adults now and no one can make you do things you don't want to do. I want to see you kids happy."

But you can never be happy with what you have, Ivy. And what you want—who you want—can he be yours?

When I didn't respond, Rosanne said, "Think about it, will you? Promise me you won't compromise on your happiness. Promise me you won't run because you're scared."

It took everything I had to hold back and not cry. I nodded. "I promise."

"Good," she smiled and patted my hand.

With that conversation out of the way, we positioned ourselves by the entrance.

The first guests arrived and for the next half hour, we were busy greeting every person who entered through the door. Xavier and Rosanne were extremely gracious in introducing me to everyone. Now all of Ryan's friends and acquaintances knew who his sister was, and that she wasn't a figment of his imagination.

Mission accomplished.

My jaw hurt from all the smiling and laughing I was doing, but it was worth it because I got to meet new people and learn who was who and how they knew Ryan.

Rosanne had given me a lot to think about, too. She had every right to say what she said and guide me in the right direction. If my mom were here, she would have agreed with every word.

If I want to be happy, I have to make peace with my past, accept my present, and look forward to my future.

"Do you mind if I run to the washroom?" I asked, needing a quick moment of alone time to compose myself.

Xavier gestured to the driveway. "We're still waiting on a few more guests, Ivy. You go ahead."

Rubbing my throat, I let the lump of pain recede. When I calmed down, I reapplied my lipstick and checked myself out in the mirror. My skin was glowing. I looked good. Actually, I looked better than ever. Maybe Rosanne and Cece were right. Maybe these parties did suit me after all.

I stepped out, shut the door behind me, and turned—only to see *him*, the man who wouldn't let me forget him even for a minute. Handsome as ever in his steel gray tux, white shirt, and black bow tie, he exuded sex from head to toe.

I had no control over my heart when we were near each other. Not that I had any control when I was far away, either. I retreated to my old trick of masking my feelings for him with annoyance and prayed that it would work.

"There is nothing going on between me and Mindy." Nick went back to the same conversation as if we were meeting after an intermission.

"So, you guys aren't fucking?"

There. I said it. It had been bothering me since yesterday and now the ball was in his court.

A tense look crossed his face, but he refrained from answering that. Unfortunately, that was all I needed to know.

It was also my cue to save myself from further heartbreak. I started to turn towards the lobby, but his voice halted me.

"Why are you always in such a rush to leave before you wrap up a conversation? Tell me: Are you in a purely platonic relationship with Mike?"

"You're right. We're both involved with other people. It makes sense to go our separate ways."

"Too bad, sweetheart, because that's not an option." He smirked and took my hand in his. "You have got to stop with this Mindy and Mike shit. Don't you get it? You don't love Mike and Mindy means nothing to me."

"Mike is a great guy," I said, more to myself than Nick; but I didn't have it in me to deny what he had said.

"So are a million other men on this earth."

"Fine. What are you suggesting? What are our options, then?" My brain was fuzzy from all of this altercation. I needed to hear what he had to say.

"There's only one option. You break up with Mike and move back to Manhattan."

"Excuse me? Are you out of your mind?

"You heard me."

"You can't tell me to uproot my life just like that." I snapped my fingers, making my point. "Besides, what about Mindy?"

"Like I told you a million times, we're not in a committed relationship."

"Does Mindy know that? You're delusional to think she's not serious about you."

"I will take care of it."

"Good. I'm still not moving."

He shot me an exasperated glare. I stood my ground.

"Fine." For once, Nick gave in. "Let's not start another argument. I want you. Now tell me what *you* want, so we can finally be on the same page about something."

The desire for him burned in my chest like a constant fire. The war that raged inside of me was too much to handle. I was done. It was impossible to hide my true feelings.

"I want you, too."

He exhaled. "Finally! Does that mean we'll be together and figure out the rest as we go?"

I didn't have an answer. He took a single step toward me. Standing inches away, he gently took me by my wrists and pulled me toward him. His hands started traveling the length of my arms until they wrapped around my neck. Tilting my head back with his thumb, his soft lips touched mine and urged me to open for him. I did, without hesitation, and his tongue took the lead. Claiming what was his. Devouring me. Exploring me.

One of his hands moved to my back and the other went to my waist, pulling me even closer. And just like that, I was his once again. There was no stopping him. No stopping us.

I burned for this man.

Wrapping my hands around him, I closed the remaining distance. Our tongues danced in unison, the electric current that ran between us intensifying with every heated stroke. It was as if, with every twist of our tongues, we wanted to prove what we meant to each other.

Our kiss deepened. Our passion strengthened. Yet somehow Nick intensified the kiss even further. He was in no rush to end this moment, and I was savoring every second of this mind-numbing experience. He was intoxicating. My body craved more. My only wish was for time to stand still.

Inhaling him, I took my fill and moaned. After years of yearning and deprivation, I wanted more than a kiss. I wanted it all.

A faraway noise pulled us out of our trance. I moved away from him on instinct, panting as I tried to pull myself together. He couldn't stand the distance between us, either. This irresistible force was drawing us closer.

A server walked into the kitchen, paying no attention to us. We looked at the man before turning our faces back to each other.

I thanked my lucky stars, and my makeup rep, that my kiss-proof lipstick didn't leave any marks.

"Why are you always hiding your scar?"

I looked down at my feet, where Nick was looking. Covered under the booties tonight was my most beloved scar.

"I don't like to share what's mine," I told him. A double-edged statement, and I hoped he would get the hint.

He smiled, giving me nothing. "I thought you'd forgotten that day."

"Have you?"

"Not a single moment of it."

"That's what I hoped to hear." Taking my hands in his, he kissed my fingers. "Because I haven't forgotten it either."

He wrapped my arm around his and possessively put his palm over my hand. We stood side-by-side and were comfortable, like we were meant to be.

And so we made our entrance. People turned to look at us and nodded as we walked past them. I had no idea where we were going or who was watching us and really, none of it mattered. I was exactly where I wanted to be.

Nick parted his lips to say something. I was quicker. "You look very handsome in a tux."

"Hmm. So it's the suit, then." A slight smile danced on his lips and the hidden dimple appeared on his right cheek.

I pulled my twitchy fingers into a fist, reining my wild desire to touch him in public and claim him as mine. "No, it's not *just* the suit." I should've lied, but I couldn't.

He looked me up and down. "And you look… do you want the truth, Miss McAlister?"

"Nothing less, Mr. Nicholas Branson."

"You look extremely fuckable tonight."

Embarrassed, I tried pulling my arm from his, but his hold tightened. "You asked for honesty, didn't you? It doesn't matter how you look or what you wear, Ivy. You always take my breath away. I've been smitten by you, and the biggest mistake I ever made was not telling you that until this very moment."

I didn't know what to say, but I knew what I felt. He enchanted me.

Chapter 14

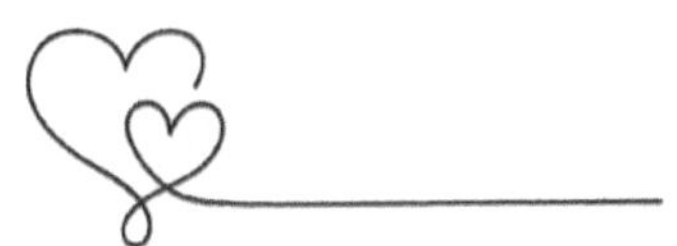

The newly engaged couple joined the crowd, looking breathtakingly gorgeous and complementing each other in every way possible. Ryan wore a black tux and Risha stunned in a champagne halter gown. Ryan's shirt matched Risha's dress, making me have faith in their stylist. Money had its own privilege.

Mom's five-carat diamond ring shone on Risha's finger, and my heart swelled with love for my brother again. He deserved all the happiness in the world. I was glad that he found *the one*.

I left Nick's side and went over to my brother and soon-to-be sister-in-law. "You two sure make a striking couple." I could barely hold back tears.

"Thanks, Ivy." Risha's smile traveled all the way to her deep brown eyes. She was glowing, almost like a bride.

"Sis! Make sure you stay away from all the men today. I don't want to get into a fight at my engagement party."

We all laughed—nervous laughter on my part—and exchanged a few more words before the others swarmed us, all wanting a moment with the guests of honor.

Leaving Ryan and Risha to mingle and chat, I headed to the bar, ordered a drink, grabbed my phone, and typed in the passcode.

Multiple messages popped up on the screen, all of them from the same person—Mike.

Hey, Ryan called me. Can you pick up?

It's getting late and you're not checking your phone. I know you're probably busy with family stuff, but I want to make sure you're okay with me coming to Ryan's engagement party tonight.

Ryan called again. I couldn't say no. I'm at my parents' house in Stamford. See you at the party.

I'm here. Where are you?

Did I have the worst luck or what?

I scanned the backyard, trying to find Mike, and silently cursed Ryan for throwing this curveball my way. I didn't need more complications in my life, and yet they kept piling up.

Yesterday, I would've been happy to see Mike. Tonight, I dreaded it.

The bartender from this afternoon placed my drink in front of me. Instead of taking a sip, I downed the entire thing in one single gulp and swept the whole place with my eyes again. There was no sign of Mike.

"What's wrong?" Nick joined me, picking up on my nervous jittering.

"Mike. My boyfriend. He's here. Apparently, Ryan invited him." I popped an olive in my mouth, my eyes darting everywhere in search of him.

The property was extensive, but everybody was here. Where was he? My heart pounding, I sent him a quick text:

I'm at the bar, on the porch.

"Break it off with him. Tonight."

My head shot up at Nick's comment.

"Ivy, I'm serious."

Finally, I spotted Mike. He was with Cece. They were searching for me.

"I need time," I told Nick.

Grabbing another cosmo even before the bartender set it down, I thanked him immensely and walked across the backyard with my heart pounding.

A nightmare in the making.

While I hugged Mike, I also thanked Cece for helping him find me. "Sorry. I just saw your messages." I started with an apology, even though since that afternoon, I'd been ignoring his messages.

"No worries." Mike looked me up and down, like Nick had done. "You look beautiful. You always do, obviously, but it's like I dropped off one version of Ivy at the airport yesterday and I'm looking at a totally different version now." He brought my hand up to his lips and kissed my fingers.

"Cece took me shopping." Feeling awkward, I half-laughed and dragged my hand away.

"What can I say? I turned Cinderella into a hot princess." Cece turned to me and added, "Honestly, you should dress up every day. No reason not to splurge when you're part of the McAlister Group and have money to spend."

Mike turned to me, surprised. "McAlister Group? Isn't that the—"

I swallowed hard, my cheeks burning. "I'll explain later."

He frowned in confusion. I put my hand on his shoulder and whispered, "Please. It's not important."

Lucky for me, he dropped the conversation. His simplicity was the first thing I liked about him. I still did. We all headed back to the bar, where Mike and Cece appeared to hit it off instantly as they got busy ordering their drinks.

With his blond hair, pale skin, soft blue eyes, and a nicely trimmed beard, my friends considered Mike handsome. I always found him a very kind-hearted man. He was more of jeans and a T-shirt kind of guy, but tonight he had gone all out in a brown suit with a beige shirt. He also wore a checkered brown-and-red tie that I had given him on his birthday. He had even gelled back his hair, something he only reserved for special occasions—like on our first date. He wasn't himself today, but he was willing to be uncomfortable if it meant making a good impression on my family.

"Break it off with him."

Nick's voice echoed inside me. I moved from one foot to another to get that thought out of my head.

Mike kissed my temple and took a sip of his drink. A gesture that would've been completely normal twenty-four hours ago suddenly felt wrong.

"So, you drove all this way for the party?" I tried to focus on anything else but his proximity.

Baffled, he knitted his eyebrows. "I told you, since you're in New York I'm spending the weekend at my parents' house in Stamford. You don't remember?"

I nodded. He did tell me that. Multiple times. At this point, Boston seemed like a distant memory.

"Ryan called this afternoon, told me he got engaged, and invited me. He thought I was in Boston and wouldn't be able to make it on such short notice, but since I was only half an hour from here... Ryan also said that he goofed things up with you and that it would make you really happy if I came."

Of course, Ryan thought that seeing my boyfriend would improve my mood. I kept a perfect smile plastered on my face while I died a little on the inside.

"How long are you staying?" Suddenly, I blanked out on our conversation.

"As long as I show up for work on Monday morning, I should be good."

"What do you do, Mike?" Cece asked, making me realize that we'd been totally ignoring her.

"I'm assisting one of my professors."

"Mike is being modest. He actually creates lesson plans for undergrad and graduate students," I told Cece. "His professor relies on him a lot because he's that good. A professor in the making."

Enjoying the praise, Mike put his right hand on my waist and pulled me closer just as Nick started approaching our group.

"I see that our last guest has arrived. Nicholas Branson," Nick announced, extending his hand to Mike.

I put some distance between me and Mike.

"Michael Schmidt. Who doesn't know you, Mr. Branson?" Leaving me, Mike shook Nick's hand. "It's nice meeting you in person."

"Pleasure is all mine. We've heard so much about you. I can't believe I'm finally getting to meet *the* Mike in person." Nick knew how to vex me, and he was going so overboard with the fake enthusiasm that even Cece noticed and gave me an eye roll.

I pinched the bridge of my nose, trying to subdue a migraine brewing behind my eyes.

"Really? I don't think Ivy ever mentioned you," Mike blurted out. Then, realizing how it sounded, he added, "Ivy's friends are my friends, though."

"How long have you been together?" Cece asked Mike.

I almost breathed. Almost.

"Two years now. Finally, we have decided to move in together. Ivy likes to take things slow," he said to the entire group.

My cheeks burned hot. The last thing I wanted to discuss in front of Nick was my living arrangement with my boyfriend.

"Yeah, she has always been a very cautious person." Nick glanced at me and said, "You're lucky that she gave you a chance."

The saliva in my mouth thickened. Thankfully, Mike was a good sport and didn't take Nick's jabs to heart.

"It's good to be cautious, I guess. And I'm definitely a lucky guy."

After Risha joined us and Cece introduced Mike, the conversation moved to Mike's doctoral program. "I can't believe all three of us studied physics!" Cece launched into a conversation filled with words I couldn't even understand.

Nick didn't contribute, but he didn't leave either. He simply stood there and stared at Mike's hand, which was back on my waist.

"I need to use the washroom," I blurted.

Everyone, including Nick, turned to look at me. Mike's attention turned to worry. He leaned in and asked softly, "Is everything okay?"

Nick's eyes burned with anger, reaching his limit. I was actually surprised it had taken him this long to nearly lose his cool. He was guarded and standoffish with strangers or people he didn't like, and his behavior at the MoxTo party proved he hadn't changed one bit.

"I had too much to drink. Need to go to the bathroom. Now."

Before Mike could offer to come with me or do anything else boyfriend-like and chivalrous in front of Nick, I covered my mouth with my hand and ran toward the house.

Bile burned a hole in my stomach from all the stress I was in. This situation felt like a bullet train heading my way and I had no control over it. All I wanted was to get through this evening, but I wasn't sure how much more stress I was up for.

I didn't really have to go to the washroom, and I definitely didn't want Nick or Mike to follow me; so I walked to the other side of the backyard where a bunch of people were standing in small groups. I drifted from one to another, mostly listening and saying very little, and laughing when everyone else laughed.

Meeting Risha's family was great. They seemed less intimidating and more friendly in reality than the image I created in my mind.

"Feeling better?" Nick's low voice filled my ear.

He was like a hot shadow I couldn't shake.

"Much better, thank you."

He pursed his lips like he knew I was never queasy to begin with. That I lied because I needed to run away like I always did.

"I want you to break up with him." Again, Nick stated his position. "Right now."

It wasn't a request. It was an order, to be exact.

And just like that, the peaceful little cocoon that I had woven around myself vanished.

I turned around, moved out of the circle of people I had been standing in, and faced him. "Don't tell me what to do," I whispered, intending for only him to hear me.

The fire in his eyes threatened to reduce me to ashes. But I had a fire of my very own. We stood there and stared at each other, neither one ready to back down—at least, not until we had company.

"Everything okay here?" Ryan's voice made my head turn. Mike, who was with him, looked from Nick to me.

"Yes, everything is fine. Nick has to return to the city for urgent work. I was asking him to wait until the dinner is over so

I can hitch a ride back." I tried to sound as convincing as possible, even though I'd made up the story on the fly.

Ryan faced Nick in surprise. "Is everything all right?"

"It's an emergency at one of the subsidiary companies," Nick answered, without going into the specifics.

I breathed a silent sigh of relief when Nick went along with my lie.

Mike, sensing the tension, chimed in. "Ivy, you can come with me to my parents' house."

I knew that Nick's eyes bored into me, but I didn't look in his direction. I couldn't. "I didn't know about Ryan's engagement until today. Tomorrow I'm meeting my school friends. I've to go back to the city tonight," I said, lying through my teeth.

"We're heading back after dinner," Nick said to no one in particular, and stormed away.

I fumbled with words to fill in the vacuum that apparently only I was noticing.

It took Ryan a few seconds to remember why he had come over. "Did you like the surprise?" he asked, giving Mike a friendly nudge—and unknowingly, getting me out of my misery.

"Definitely surprised," I said. "Thank you for inviting Mike."

"I told you I'd make it up to you." Ryan's intentions were good. It wasn't his fault that my feelings for Mike had taken a one-hundred-eighty-degree turn since I reconnected with Nick.

Mike wrapped his arm around my waist, making my body go stiff. He felt the tension and moved immediately.

I wasn't mad at Mike. Just like Ryan, he had done nothing wrong. I was irritated with myself. I took Mike's hand in mine to show him that everything was okay.

And waited for this ordeal to end.

Chapter 15

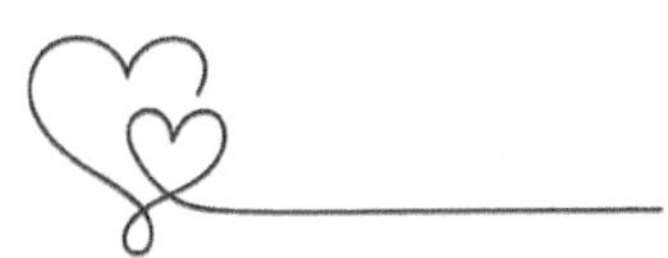

When dinner was announced, Mike and I followed the other guests. A long wooden table held centerpieces constructed out of sunflowers and candles. There were rows of chairs on both sides of the table. Strings of fairy lights overhead illuminated the place. The backyard had been transformed into a cozy, rustic Tuscan retreat. Two words described it: romantic and breathtaking.

Like my mother, who had always made it her mission to plan the coolest themed parties, Rosanne had made everything perfect for Ryan and Risha.

I held back tears, silently thanking the universe for bringing Rosanne and Xavier—our guardian angels—into our lives. Their son, though, was a different story altogether.

I was admiring all the little details when I heard Mike say, "You look gorgeous tonight."

He leaned in to kiss me. Instinctively, I did something I had never done before—I moved back.

Realization hit him. Something was wrong, and he knew it.

My behavior confused him. And me as well. Deep down, I had changed. It was like I'd been tossed into some parallel universe as soon as I landed in New York. Whatever it was, I didn't know how to control my feelings for Nick or how to explain things to Mike.

Mike and I had a history. He was always there for me when I needed him. He did everything in his power to make me happy and expected nothing in return. Uncomfortable he might be in his party attire, yet he was here, at this party, with me and for me.

With guilt tearing up my insides, I leaned in and kissed him—kissed him for all the times he had been there for me, for tolerating all of my quirks, and especially for all the great times we had had together.

Not knowing that the kiss was the beginning of an end, Mike relaxed, wrapped his arm around me, and kissed me back. Our kiss was passionate, the way we had kissed in the past; but I wasn't into it anymore. I wasn't sure if I felt sorry for us or hated myself at that moment. All I really wanted was for this evening to end.

When we broke apart, I instantly felt Nick's furious gaze on me. I had to end this madness somehow. To untangle myself from the mess I had created around me.

Nick sat as far away from me as possible and refused to look in my direction. I didn't know how to justify my actions. I had strong feelings for one, but I was someone else's girlfriend.

"You haven't been yourself today," Mike said, once the people at the table fell into a lively conversation.

"I have a terrible headache."

"I know you don't like to bother anyone, but tell me what I can do to make you feel better. You know I'll do anything for you."

After everything I had done, his kindness hurt. "Don't worry about me. It's nothing some quality sleep won't fix."

"Are you sure you want to go back to New York with a stranger, instead of driving up to my parents' house with me?"

"I told you. I have plans with friends in the city. And Nicholas isn't a stranger. He's a… a family friend," I responded, with irritation.

"And I'm your boyfriend," he reminded me.

"I know." It was a non-answer, but Mike decided not to push it.

After the dessert round, the guests started leaving the table. We did the same. Despite my odd behavior, Mike offered me his hand and helped me up.

During our two years together, we had never had a fight or a disagreement… but all of that was going to change tonight.

"Ivy, are you not going to introduce me to this young gentleman?" Xavier stopped us when he saw us skirting around the side of the table. "Xavier Branson." He pushed his hand forward.

"Mike Schmidt. Ivy's boyfriend," he said, affirming our relationship. Both men shook hands. "Thank you for having me over. It was a beautiful party."

"Glad you could join us. Ivy is like a daughter to us. You better be treating her right." It looked like Xavier wanted to say more or ask something. "Give some thought to the discussion we had this afternoon, Ivy," was all he said before he gave Mike a stern pat on the shoulder and went back to smoking his cigar.

"That man hates me," Mike said, as soon as we were alone in the driveway.

"Who? Xavier? He doesn't hate you."

"Yes, he does. And you didn't say anything to change his mind. Honestly, I thought I knew you. But right now it feels like I just met you for the first time."

"What do you mean?" I sounded more defensive than I meant to.

His eyes fixed on me. I could tell he was holding himself back. We have never argued before.

"Did Ryan make a mistake by inviting me? Clearly, you don't want me here."

"To be honest, Mike, seeing you here took me by surprise. I wasn't expecting you. That's all."

"So, he *did* make a mistake?"

"That's not what I meant. It's just that…" I didn't know how to confess without hurting his feelings. How was I supposed to explain I wanted to end a two-year relationship after spending twenty-four hours with my teenage crush? "Maybe you're right. Maybe you don't really know me."

"I realized that today. McAlister Group, expensive clothes, fancy parties, folks like Xavier Branson… I'm trying to figure out why you left it all behind. But if you never told me about your life outside of Boston, it means you don't trust me."

I've been living a lie, pretending to be someone I'm not. Even worse, if Nick tells me to jump, I will ask, "How high?" But that has nothing to do with me not trusting you.

I wanted to say all of that and more, but the words knotted in my throat.

Mike's voice broke through my internal musings. "Ivy, I don't know what's going on with you but don't make any hasty decisions. Let's talk when you return. Okay?"

"Okay," was all I managed before the valet pulled up in Mike's car, got out, and handed him the keys.

I watched him get in and squeeze the steering wheel hard. "Call me when you're ready."

I stood there and tracked his car as it sped down the road. Then he made a turn and I couldn't see it anymore.

———————————————

By the time I returned, the party was winding down. As much as I tried to take part in the conversations and have fun, the anxiety wouldn't leave me.

My life was in shambles. How had this happened in such a short time?

At some point, Ryan, Risha, and Cece joined us. "Can I get your number, Ivy?" Cece asked. "Let's hang out in the city next."

I agreed. After I exchanged my numbers with Cece and Risha, Rosanne reminded me that she was looking forward to getting a call from me, too. I took the hint and promised not to be a stranger.

My phone vibrated in my hand. I turned it around to see if Abby was calling, only to find the battery at a ten percent charge. With a mental note to charge it as soon as I reach home, I dropped my phone back into my clutch.

Nick joined us and stood beside me. I tried to disguise my nerves as best I could, but I wasn't sure it was working.

"Ready to head out?" he asked me.

"Yeah. I need to grab my stuff and say bye to some people. See you in fifteen?"

"Meet me in the driveway." He turned and started talking to Taber.

When I returned with my bag in hand, Nick kissed Risha on the cheek and fist-bumped Ryan. A steward ran up and reached for my bag.

"I've got it," Nick stopped him.

"As you wish, Mr. Branson."

A few more cheek kisses and handshakes later, Nick shoved the bag in the trunk and we were back inside his Lamborghini.

I didn't even have time to put on my seatbelt before he was zooming out of the driveway and heading for the main road.

Chapter 16

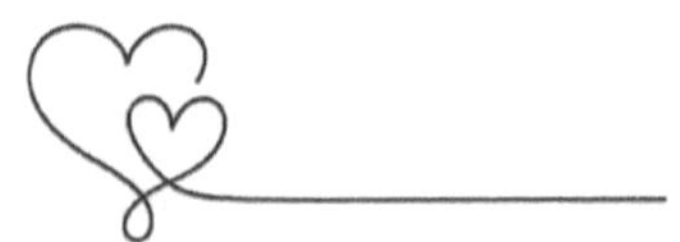

Nick drove like a maniac. Lucky for us, there were no cops patrolling the roads or we would've been in some serious trouble.

He didn't say a word to me. I stayed quiet as well. My head spun from the way the day had unfolded and my brain wasn't capable of handling any more emotional rollercoasters.

Convincing myself that I wasn't at fault, I tried to relax.

Mike is your boyfriend. Or would saying "was" be closer to the truth?

What would I have done if he'd kissed Mindy or Celine in front of me?

Fuck!

Twenty minutes of road rage later, I got used to the silence. If Nick continued to drive like this, I'd be home sooner than I expected. Which was what I wanted, anyway.

I leaned back, closed my eyes, and let the snippets of recent events unfold. Me walking into MoxTo with Ryan. Nick ignoring me, introducing me, and then kissing me on the terrace…

The car screeched and came to a sudden stop. My eyes flew open as I jumped up, convinced that we'd gotten into an accident.

Instead, I found that we were sitting in a deserted beach parking lot.

Nick switched off the engine and faced me. *"What. Were. You. Thinking. Tonight?"* His voice boomed, filling the quiet of the car and making me jump.

"What. Do. You. Mean?" I screamed right back, trying to mimic his volume. I wasn't even close.

"Didn't I tell you to break off with Mike? And what did you do instead? You kissed him!"

I could feel his rage even in the dim glow of the light. Most people would've backed down, but I had no plans to submit to his wishes. Did he seriously think he could tell me what to do? "Sorry to break it to you. But I don't take orders from you."

His temper was reaching a boiling point. I wasn't too far from exploding myself. Muttering something under his breath, Nick came closer. He pulled me by my forearm and firmly put his lips on mine, forcing his tongue inside my mouth as if attempting to erase the memories of the evening.

Shocked by this sudden force, I shut my lips and attempted to push him away. Typically, the physical force would've turned me on, but now I found it repulsive.

He was relentless. I held my ground. When I didn't give in to his insistence, his lips started traveling to the rest of my face, my eyes, my neck, and even my hair. Too stunned to process any of this, I continued to resist his strength.

"Stop, Nick. Stop! You've got to stop."

"Don't fight me, Ivy." His voice was filled with pain and with longing. He was aching for me. "Please don't fight me."

"I can't do this." My heart had been in a battle all day. I wasn't sure I could take any more. My past and present, my fantasies and my reality, were all colliding. It was bewildering. It was dizzying.

Nick heard my plea and came to a halt, but refused to release his grip. Maintaining our physical contact, he leaned his head against my shoulder. His lips brushed my neck as a tornado brewed inside my heart. My hand remained on his chest, counting his unsteady heartbeats.

I was drawn to him. I wanted to run away. Indecision clouded my thoughts.

Your wants and needs are the same, Ivy. It's Nick. It has always been Nick.

"We need to talk." He kissed me on the forehead and sat up straight.

Then he got out of the car, came over to my side, and opened the door. I put my hand in his and got out without arguing.

"Let's take a walk."

As we strolled across the deserted parking lot, the wind gently tussled the loose strands of my hair. The cool air carried the familiar humidity of this time of the year. Sparse streetlights provided a glow in the otherwise dark night. I focused on all the mundane things around us to calm my nerves.

Before getting on the boardwalk, I paused to remove my shoes. Nick waited with me, both of us scared to disturb the peace—this perfect moment of lull—after coming out of a wild storm.

I took one shoe in each hand and started walking barefoot. A short distance later, we reached the stairs that led to the beach. He gestured to me to take those steps and I did, with no objection. Our walk was helping me. It was helping us.

Instead of going toward the rolling waves, we stayed closer to the boardwalk and continued our walk. The cooling sensation of sand under my feet calmed my nerves. Although it was a little chilly, I realized I could walk all night as long as Nick walked beside me.

"I went to Boston. Many times."

Stunned, I halted. He stayed quiet, letting his words sink in.

In Boston, I had felt his presence many times, but I always assumed my imagination was playing tricks on me. I had been so obsessed with Nick that the idea of seeing him everywhere I went didn't seem that far-fetched.

"I worked in our Boston office and stayed there on and off." He tugged at me slightly, encouraging me to keep walking. "You were a kid, Ivy. Not to mention that you were also Ryan's sister. I wanted you to come back to Manhattan, hoping you would get over your obsession with Boston and move back."

"Why didn't you ever meet me?"

"And say what to you?"

"Say what you said to me tonight—that you wanted me. Why did you wait all these years?"

"You were a minor, Ivy. I would've never crossed that line."

"And what about when I wasn't a minor?" I huffed, realizing that our age gap was a legitimate issue. A barrier he had to get over.

Ignoring my question, Nick continued. "After a while, Dad insisted I stay in New York and take over the business. He was eager to retire and he wanted me to be ready for the handover. You were coming for the holidays. I planned to confess my feelings and ask you to come back to Manhattan, but then Ryan told me about Harvard and how you weren't coming back. I was so upset that I found Celine and brought her home with me that night."

"Wow," was all I could say. I couldn't believe my ears.

He continued. "I started getting involved at work. Life happened and I tried to move on. Women always came and went, but no one could make me forget you. You were my best friend's sister, a decade younger, and moving on with your life. Even though I knew there was no way we could ever be together, I still couldn't stop thinking about you."

"Nick…"

"Let me finish," he interrupted. "Last year when Ryan visited you, I was there with him."

"You already told me that. You didn't even bother to come see me."

"I did come, Ivy. But I saw you introducing Mike to Ryan… and you seemed happy."

You are such a fool.

"And I let you go until you decided to show up here." Nick turned toward me. "But now that you're here, I can't ignore my feelings. I can't keep living my life not knowing what's going on between us and how far it can go."

My mind was reeling. *All these years of thinking about Nick, trying to forget him, and looking for someone—anyone—to replace him with… and he felt the same way about me the entire time.*

My heart had no space for anyone else. Thoughts of him consumed my brain. I wasn't proud of it, but I even thought about him while having sex with other guys. Little did I know he had been thinking of me all this time.

I stood there, processing his admission. My chest hurt from the intense pain that only one person could inflict, but I didn't want to think about how unhappy his absence had made me for years. Honestly, I didn't want to think at all.

I wrapped my arms around Nick's neck and tugged him closer. Our intense attraction sparked when his lips crashed into mine. His kiss, powerful and demanding, was laced with deep longing and with deep yearning. With each stroke of his tongue, he told me what I meant to him, and I did the same.

Our repressed need for one another came out in waves. I didn't want to stop. I was his, and he was mine.

His mouth traveled down my chin, leaving a string of wet, ardent kisses on my skin. His fingers started unbuttoning the front of my dress and before I knew it, Nick had some competition because the chilly wind was kissing my bare skin. Fire and goosebumps covered every part of me. Hunger and thirst won't let me breathe. Right here, right now, it was only me and Nick.

We sat down on the sand. Nick was in front of me, kissing me and gently touching the scar on my ankle. He took my hand in his and laid a soft kiss against my palm. I took his hand and did the same. Our eyes met and just like that, without having to say a single word, we confessed our love for each other.

Nick kissed every inch of my exposed skin, the throbbing pain between my legs getting more and more unbearable by the second. It was the same pain that I'd been living with for years.

I moaned as his mouth rubbed over my panties. Breathing out hot breath, I was on fire. My body ached. My heartbeat was out of control.

"I want you."

"Are you sure?" he asked between the kisses.

"Yes," I said without any hesitation in my voice. I'd never wanted anyone else the way I wanted Nick now.

He ran the tip of his nose up and down my folds. Pleasure sparked, flooding every cell of my being. He took a deep inhale and growled. Pulled my panties down and out of the way, he moaned in approval. "Hope you didn't wax it recently. I don't want to hurt you."

"You can never hurt me, Nick. But I'm impressed with your knowledge of bikini waxing."

A hoarse laugh ripped through his chest. "Thanks. I might know a thing or two."

Gripping my thighs, he lashed his tongue over my clitoris. A shudder ran through my core. His assault continued. I grew wetter and more aroused than ever as I allowed Nick to take me to a new realm of pleasure.

"I want you, Nick. All of you," I begged. My breathy voice didn't sound like mine.

"I can't. Don't have a condom." I heard his voice through the onslaught of pleasure.

"Please, Nick… I'm on birth control and I got tested a few weeks ago. I'm clean. I promise."

He stopped and looked at me. I pleaded with my eyes.

"I've never had sex without a condom," he told me. "I get myself tested regularly, too, promise you don't have to worry about it. But are you completely sure that I can be inside you?" He sounded almost desperate, yet waiting for my approval. Keeping his desires in check by only a thread. "I want you badly, but I won't do anything that you don't want me to do."

"I want you, too. Desperately."

That was all he needed to lay me down on the sand and get out of his pants, his long, hard cock on display. I was in awe. I hadn't seen anything so big and beautiful before.

"Don't worry. I won't hurt you."

"I know you won't. Nick, I have waited so long…"

His eyes filled with something I could only describe as love. Boxing me in between his arms, he put his weight on his elbow, bent down, and kissed me softly… making me taste my own arousal. His rock-hard cock pressed between us, maddening me with a need I had never felt for anyone else.

"We both have, sweetheart."

Moving my legs apart, he made space for himself. Positioned beneath him, I squirmed in anticipation when I felt his hard erection nudging the lip of my sex.

"Are you sure you want to do this?" he asked again.

"Yes, damn it! Do you want me to sign a permission slip or what?"

His loud, husky laugh filled the space between us and seeped deep into my heart. I was wet, needy, and ready for him as his hard, throbbing erection made its way inside me.

Slowly, gently, he made space for himself. He entered. Lightning traveled through my veins. Our connection was so strong that I held my breath. Nick stopped.

"Do you feel it?" he asked, breathless. I couldn't talk. I had never felt like this before.

Nick garbled some words that I couldn't understand. I was floating in my ecstasy. After filling me completely, he set the tempo, building a slow, even rhythm. I savored the moment, wanting nothing more than to commit every second to memory.

His hands started kneading my breasts. He sucked on my nipples one at a time, my relentless need for him torturous and pleasurable at the same time.

Nick moved his head to look me in the eye. "You're mine," he growled.

Pleasure started roaring through me, igniting me, and ready to explode inside of me. As my core clenched, I noted his quickened heartbeat.

"You feel this too, baby, don't you?"

"Of course I do. How can I not?" I breathed out.

"I've ached for you for years, Ivy."

"And I've waited so long to hear these words. So long that I almost gave up all hope."

Even in the darkness, I could see into the depths of his soul. He wanted me as much as I wanted him. I wasn't the only one suffering. And I surely wasn't the only one waiting.

So close to my release, I could barely speak. "I'm going to… come," I forced out, my voice hoarse.

Nick looked deep into my eyes. Our desires were attuned.

I heard his voice through a fog of passion. "Now, sweetheart. Come with me *now*."

Totally undone by him, I broke into the tiniest of particles. His release followed in succession, and I kept wringing him until the last drop of him was inside of me.

Chapter 17

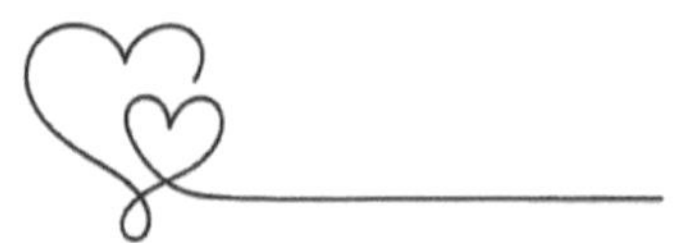

The moonlit night was telling a story of its own, with waves crashing in the distance and playing a soothing melody. Time meant nothing as we lay next to each other under the stars and enjoyed each other's warmth. Every fiber of my being was aware of Nick's presence. My world outside of his embrace didn't exist. I didn't want this moment to end.

I still couldn't believe that he wanted me as much as I wanted him. It felt like another one of my dreams, and yet it was my new reality.

All these years we wasted… all and the time we lost. *But now what?*

One after another, questions started popping into my mind. *What does Nick want to happen? What should I do next?*

The moment of clarity faded, leaving me confused and lost once again.

My hands moved around his arms. I snuggled into him. When my fingers reached the scar on his biceps, I asked, "How bad was the pain?"

"Not as bad as seeing you in pain."

"You were in far worse shape than me. I was afraid of losing you forever because of all the blood loss." From my memory, I saw that dreaded hospital bed and his pale face.

"You took care of me even with your broken ankle, Ivy. Made the nurses' lives hell until they moved you into my room. You stayed with me until my family showed up at the hospital the next morning. And you even kept mom and dad calm even though you were in pain. I haven't forgotten anything."

"You were going in and out of consciousness. It scared me to death, Nick. And it was my fault for insisting on riding bikes in that weather when everybody told me it was a terrible idea."

He smiled at me. "I couldn't say no to you twice in one day. It was my motorbike or that. I had to pick the lesser of the evils."

I laughed, thinking of that morning. It was a day etched into my memory like it had happened yesterday. I was sixteen. It was the last notable holiday I had with him.

At some point, we got up and put our clothes back on in silence. Nick tugged me into him and kissed the crown of my head. "Are you cold?" he asked.

When I nodded, he draped his jacket to cover my bare front and wrapped his arm around my waist. We intertwined our fingers and headed back to the car.

"What are we going to do, Nick?" I could not resist asking the pressing question of the moment.

"Let's explore this and see where it leads us."

"I want that too, but I can't leave Boston. It's my home."

"About that… I can't leave everything I have going on in the city. It would be so much easier for you to move."

My irritation returned. I already disliked where this discussion was headed. "So, you're saying your work is important and my life is not?"

"That's not what I'm saying." Annoyance was evident in his voice. "Besides, you can do everything in New York that you're doing in Boston."

"My friends, my school, my life as I know it…they are all in Boston. I can't get up and leave because you're asking me to."

"Your family is *here*, Ivy, not in Boston. Even your professor has moved here. What do you want to go back for?"

Is Nick seriously telling me how to live my life?

"Boston is where I belong now. I can't leave everything and move without giving it some serious thought. And I won't," I said, with finality.

Nick's phone rang, halting us both. He picked up the phone without taking his eyes off of me. "Not now," he said to whoever was on the other end, and hung up.

We each opened our car door and got in. I threw his jacket on the backseat and strapped my seatbelt on.

"Why are you here, Ivy? Why did you decide to come back after all these years?"

"I… I don't know. I wasn't expecting to see you when I booked my ticket, if that's what you're insinuating." I was annoyed by his presumption.

The engine came to life, and we started driving. Minutes passed by before his voice filled the car again. "It's up to you if you want to give us a chance or not. I can only tell you this: what we have comes few and far between."

"And what happens when it fizzles out?"

"Do you seriously think that's possible?"

"The only thing I know is that I'm not ready to leave Boston. I've made a life there for myself. More importantly, I can be anonymous in Boston. That will end as soon as I make New York my permanent home." I was talking more to myself than to Nick.

"Your anonymity is already gone. I couldn't stop the pictures of you and Ryan from coming out."

I sighed, knowing he was right; but I couldn't turn my life upside down just because he told me to. If this was going to work, I needed to have some agency in the relationship.

Unfortunately, we had both reached an impasse. We stayed quiet for the rest of the drive and, at some point, I drifted off to sleep.

When I opened my eyes, we were already in Manhattan. Nick had parked near Ryan's building and was typing furiously on his phone.

"Sorry. I fell asleep," I said groggily, as I sat up straight. "How long have you been waiting?"

"That's all right." Nick removed his seatbelt and exited the car.

I found the shoes that I hadn't bothered to put on since I took them off for our stroll along the boardwalk. Once I was decent, I got out of the car, too.

Nick was already removing my bag from the trunk. The vibe coming from him was nothing short of chilly and withdrawn, making me feel like I didn't know him at all. Was he the same man who had chased me all day, said that he wanted me, and gotten lost in an intimate moment with me?

Unable to process my feelings and his indifference, I took my bag from his hand and turned to go inside the building. At this moment, I needed to be as far away from him as possible.

Nick tugged on my bag and pulled me toward him. I couldn't read him at all and he wasn't talking, which made the entire situation even more confusing. He looked into my eyes. The desire I had seen in his eyes earlier was gone.

His phone buzzed again, making me wonder who had been trying to reach him in the middle of the night. Nick didn't pick up, nor did he give any explanation.

"Let's talk in the morning," was all he said. Then he kissed me on the forehead, got back into the car, and drove off.

Distant, distracted, and detached, I couldn't shake the feeling that Nick was already done with me. Maybe that was his plan all along. Drive me insane, get me to have sex with him, and then throw in a condition he knew I would never agree to. Now he'd had his fun and washed his hands of me without any mess.

The stupid pain of betrayal was growing deeper with every passing moment. Missing his touch and his presence, and with my heart in turmoil, I wasn't sure how to pull myself together. Instead of going inside the building, I started walking down the street with no particular destination in mind. Once I got tired and cold, I hailed a cab and had the driver drop me off at a familiar place.

Although it was one of the busiest train stations in the country, tonight Penn Station looked almost deserted. I sat on a bench and contemplated my options. The movement all around reminded me that I was wrong. This was New York City, the city that never sleeps, and the Pennsylvania train station where trains run twenty-four-seven. And thanks to my outfit, I was standing out like a sore thumb and getting stared at.

What a lovely way to end my night.

After sitting alone and wallowing in my sorrows for what felt like forever, I finally called the only person I could turn to. Five rings later Abby picked up.

"Ivy?" Her woozy voice was filled with concern. *"What's going on?"*

There was no stopping me now. As soon as I heard her voice, all hell broke loose. I wasn't someone who cried easily, but I ended up sobbing until I felt numb. I was back to where I started—heartbroken and rejected by the same man once again.

I had learned how to take care of my broken heart, but now I'd lost years of learning and in just one night. I wished I could tell Abby everything, but it hurt too much and the words wouldn't form.

"Whatever happened, Ivy, please don't cry. You're stronger than this."

"And what if I'm not?" I said, choking on my tears. A lady turned her entire body to look at me, but I didn't care.

"You're one of the strongest women I know. I look up to you. Don't sell yourself short. Now, listen carefully to what I'm about to say."

When I put down the phone, I was already on autopilot and doing exactly what Abby had told me to do. I found an empty bathroom stall, locked it, and changed out of the dress I was wearing. Then I slipped on my jeans, put on the white top I had worn earlier, washed my face, walked back out with my dress draped over my arm, and bought a ticket at one of the vending machines.

Destination: Boston.

I was about to stuff my dress in my bag when I saw a girl around my age admiring the dress. In leggings and a simple top and jean jacket, she looked ordinary—but only because her clothes weren't doing her beauty any justice.

"Hi," I said.

"Hi."

"First time in this city?"

She blushed. "Is it that obvious?" She tucked a strand of hair behind her ear, just like I had a habit of doing. "I came to New York to see my boyfriend who I haven't seen in a year. We're both from Virginia, but he got a job in the city while I stayed back home to finish school and save up some money. Now that he's settled in and I got a few days off, he wants to show me the city and introduce me to his friends."

Seemed like she wanted to talk. I had time to listen.

"Here, take it," I handed her the dress.

She hesitated. "Are you sure?"

"You're beautiful without it, but you will make a killer first impression with it on."

She took the dress from me and carefully felt the fabric, like it was the most exquisite thing she had ever touched. From the story she told me, she couldn't afford anything that expensive and I had no plans to wear this dress again. She had come here to spend time with her boyfriend and impress his friends. I was certain she was going to make better use of it than I ever would.

I fished around my bag until I found the accessories that matched and handed them to her as well. She thanked me profusely and hugged me. I let her. Helping her made me forget my pain, even if for a little while.

"Is your boyfriend coming to pick you up?" I wanted to make sure she wasn't wasting her time on some jerk like I did.

"He called me, actually. He's parked right outside."

"Good," I smiled back at her. "Enjoy the city and the dress."

After giving her the directions, I went to my designated platform and waited for the train. A short moment later, I got on an early morning train to Boston.

Once I arrived, I bought another ticket and headed to a place where I'd spent some of my best holidays and summers. I was ready to heal my heart all over again.

Chapter 18

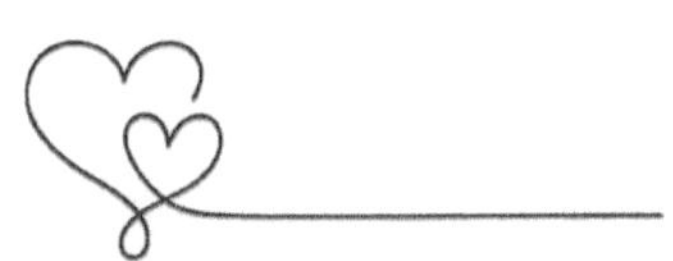

Abby waved to get my attention as soon as I exited the train station in Marlborough, Massachusetts. She was going for a casual look today in a blue sundress and a high ponytail. A beautiful brunette with powder blue eyes, the same height as me with a matching slender figure, we'd been mistaken for sisters on more occasions than one.

We embraced. But unlike our conversation last night, I didn't cry—a fact I was pretty proud of, given the circumstances. I put my bag in the trunk of her beaten down sedan and sat in the front passenger seat.

"Why were you working on Saturday?" I asked, attempting to talk about lighter topics as I buckled up. "And why are you here when you should be in the apartment, using this weekend to pack?"

As much as I loved Abby, she was the biggest procrastinator I had ever met. She was leaving for California in a few weeks, but the only thing she had done was buy a few cardboard moving boxes.

"After a very emotional lecture from Dad, I thought it'd be easier to spend the weekend with them than pack. Mom asked me to take Monday off. That's why I had to work on Saturday."

To keep my mind occupied, I asked her to fill me in on all the ways her parents had tried to convince her to stay. They weren't happy with Abby's decision to move to the other side of the country, but while Abby loved Boston, she loved Parker more and wouldn't live here without him.

Since Abby was the oldest of three siblings and her parents' favorite, it was no surprise that Roger and Beth were having a hard time accepting the change. According to them, Parker could've easily chosen a program in Boston; but since his parents were from San Diego, he chose UCLA instead. Abby had made her decision as soon as he got in.

I couldn't blame Abby's parents for reacting this way. I still remembered how my mother was in tears when Ryan went to college, even though he was in the same city and visiting home often. Abby's parents and I met once we became roommates and best friends in our sophomore year of college. Her family had accepted me with open arms.

Only Abby and her parents knew who I really was, but they never brought up my family's wealth. They loved me for me and not for the money that I had.

By the time we reached Abby's house, which was only a brief car ride away, breakfast was already on the table. The scrumptious smell of bacon and eggs made my stomach grumble so loud that her parents heard it even before I set foot into the kitchen.

After breakfast, I poured myself a second cup of coffee. Then Abby and I headed to the backyard and sat on the swings under our favorite red maple tree. She adjusted herself on the swing next to me.

There used to be one swing on this tree earlier. When Roger noticed how much we loved spending time here, he added another one. He told us it was our summer present.

I had grown accustomed to this life. It was peaceful and free. Now, the warm summer morning in New England welcomed me with bright sunlight, the smell of freshly cut grass, and the sound of bees buzzing around the rose bushes. The vibrant begonias and the chrysanthemums chipped away at the heavy feelings I'd been carrying with me since last night.

"Are you ready to talk now?" Abby watched me intently and took a few sips of coffee as we both sat still on the swings. She couldn't hide her concern any longer.

I sighed. "To be honest, I don't even know where to start."

"Just tell me what's eating you, Ivy."

"I had sex with someone last night."

"You did *what?*" she asked, her eyes wide.

I was expecting this horrified look, and more, because it was so unlike me. I had only been in a few relationships that quickly fizzled out. I was never one to jump into a man's bed or, in this case, roll around with him in the sand.

"Is this what you wanted to talk about when you texted yesterday morning?"

"I kissed the same guy the day I landed in New York. And the chain of events led to... you know."

"Are you crazy?" She got that part right.

Nick has always been my weakness, and my lust for him made me temporarily lose my mind. But I didn't know how to tell Abby that. "I know you think I'm this cautious person who doesn't jump into things without thinking them through, but..."

"No, that's the opposite of what I think," she insisted. "I think you've been hiding. Trying to be someone you're not. And you know this is not the first time we've had this conversation. Every time I bring up the fact that you should live a little, you make a face and shut me down."

I nodded. Once again, she was right.

"You think I don't know you. But in actuality, I know you better than you think I do."

"That's good. Because I'm not sure who I am anymore. Or what I want."

Abby set her cup down on the grass. "Focus on one thing at a time and tell me what's going through your mind. We can work through this together."

Inhaling, I pushed the air out through my mouth and began. "I feel terrible for cheating on Mike. Trust me, I never intended to hurt him. And I know once he finds out, he's going to be crushed." With the back of my hand, I quickly wiped the tears that were streaming down my face. "He doesn't deserve this, Abby. Mike has been nothing but good to me. Now I'm thinking that maybe I shouldn't have gone to New York at all." I pushed through the glob of pain in my throat that was ready to suffocate me.

"Cheating is never the answer. I get that. But Ivy… we both know you don't love Mike."

I cocked my head to the side.

"Don't look so surprised. We've gone over this many times. Your 'I will fall in love with him eventually' theory doesn't hold up. You are only *content* with him. You don't *love* him and you never did."

"He has always been so kind to me. And nothing can justify cheating on him."

"Agreed. That's why I was so shocked to hear that you did. But I also know you would never intentionally hurt anyone. If you cheated on him, there's more to it that you're not telling me." She asserted her point. "At least accept the truth—you and Mike don't belong together. You are forcing yourself to love him. If it didn't happen in two years, it won't happen. Ever."

"I'm content with my life, Abby. In Boston. With Mike. Life is easy and uncomplicated here."

"Are you listening to yourself? You're settling for the life of an old lady before you've even had a chance to really *live*." Her voice rose. "Wake up! Be bold! Take risks. Get hurt. Let Mike go and do something you've never done before."

She had never been this blunt with me and I wasn't sure how to take it, so I got up from the swing and started walking toward the house. She quietly followed me.

"Who *is* this other guy?" she asked in a mellow voice.

"A nobody." I quickened my pace and left Abby outside.

Picking up my bag from the foyer where I had left it earlier, I walked up a single flight of stairs to Abby's room. Up there, I pulled my jogging shorts and T-shirt out of the bag and headed for the bathroom.

My plan was to take a quick shower to see if it would help me get rid of the exhaustion and stress. Unfortunately, when I took off my hairpin and sand started coming out of my hair, it once again reminded me of Nick and the time we had spent together last night.

Tears ran down my face. There was no stopping them.

I chose him even though I knew this was where I would land. One step forward and ten steps back. Today I was exactly where I was four years ago. Miserable. Hurting. And missing Nick madly.

When I opened the bathroom door, Abby was waiting for me in the hallway in shorts, a Harvard T-shirt, and running shoes. "I'll join you."

She really knew me well.

We walked to a quiet part of town and alternated between jogging and fast walking for the next few hours, without talking to each other. Running made me content. I needed this—the peace and quiet—rather than the emotional highs and lows I was dealing with.

The sun kept rising, but we went on.

Eventually, when we reached our favorite park and ran two more laps, I fell onto the grass and quit. Not enough sleep and feeling guilty over juggling two men was taking a toll on my emotional wellbeing.

Abby sat down not far from me, equally exhausted, and took her Bluetooth out of her ears. I guzzled down half of the water from my bottle before I handed it to her. She finished the rest and playfully tossed the empty bottle at me, which I—caught off guard—failed to catch. It hit me in the head and it made us both laugh.

"We need to work on your reflexes."

"There's a lot more than poor reflexes that I need to fix."

Abby scooted over to me. "Okay. Now, tell me about this guy."

I focused on a gray catbird circling the tree to stop myself from crying. "His name is Nick. He's Ryan's best friend. After my parents died, Nick's parents became our guardians."

"You never mentioned anything about him."

"I wanted to forget him."

There was nothing else to do but tell Abby the truth. I opened up about our past and our present until I arrived at our disagreement about Boston and Nick's subsequent cold shoulder.

"It sounds like he's already got you convinced. You just don't want to admit it to yourself," Abby started as soon as I finished. "Besides, like I told you: Mike is a great guy, but he is not *your* guy."

"I thought you were happy that Mike and I were moving in together."

"As roommates. But not as a couple because these are two very different things. I want you to love the man you're with as much as I love Parker. Like you won't be able to survive another day without him. Like you can fight the entire world just to be with him. Have you ever felt like that?"

Yes. Every time I think about Nick.

"That doesn't happen in real life." I walked over to pick up the empty water bottle.

Abby followed me. "It happened to me. It happened to Ryan. At least give yourself a chance, is all I am saying."

"You don't even know Nick. Maybe all he wanted was sex."

"I don't need to know Nick to tell you that Mike is not the right person for you. Don't get me wrong, I'm not rooting for Nick here. And I like Mike. But you're my friend and I want to see you happy, alive, and excited about life, and you haven't been any of those things for a very long time now." Abby looked up at me. "Don't fear getting hurt, Ivy. That is all I'm saying. It's all part of finding our happiness."

When I didn't respond, she asked another question. "Are you happy? Truly happy?"

"No." I couldn't lie anymore. "I am not happy here."

"See? You've all the answers within you. Now, do yourself a favor and be truthful to yourself. Do you love Nick?"

Yes! Yes! Yes!

"No." I masked my feelings behind a what-the-hell look. "I want to be with him. Always have. But I don't know him well enough to love him."

"Has he been in touch with you since he dropped you off?"

"Knowing our history, it's highly unlikely that he will ever touch base with me again."

"That's your assumption. When was the last time you checked your phone?"

"It's not… I'm not ready to be disappointed again. Besides, he wanted me to move to Manhattan. I told him I wouldn't. Pretty sure that was a deal-breaker for him." Throwing the empty bottle in the trash, I did some stretches while Abby mulled over what I had said.

"Would it really be so bad?" She was giving this discussion more thought than I had. "I mean, have you thought about what you want out of life? You wanted to get into Harvard, and you did. Wanted to get into the MBA program, and you got in. Wanted to be in Professor Sinclair's class, and you got that too. What's next? Are you sure the plan beyond that doesn't include New York and Nick?"

"You're wrong on that last one. Professor Sinclair is going to be teaching at Columbia next semester." I updated her on that as well.

Why not give her the complete picture of how my world is slowly falling apart?

She looked at me inquisitively as I filled her in on my conversation with the professor at the MoxTo opening.

"Okay. Please help me understand. If the professor is in New York and the guy you're crazy about is also there, why do you want to stay here?"

"Honestly, I don't like people telling me what to do. And the truth is, I don't even know if Nick is into me on a deep level or if it's purely physical. For all I know, there's no truth to anything he told me over these last few days." I tried with all my might to keep myself from crying.

"I get that you're confused. But how will you know for sure unless you talk to him? And seriously—if it's not Nick, it will be someone else, but it's definitely not Mike. Can we at least agree on that?"

"Fine. You've made your point." Hunching down, I started making my way toward the soccer field where Abby's brother was playing. This wasn't the first time we'd discussed my relationship with Mike, but now she had the reason to prove why I shouldn't be with him. "Do you mind if we change the subject?"

As much as I had hoped that talking things out would help me get rid of these nagging feelings, it was only making them worse.

There is no one but Nick, Ivy. Even if he's not serious, you would rather be with him for a day than an entire life with someone else. Accept it.

Abby hugged me from behind. "Absolutely. Promise me you'll think about what I said, okay?"

I nodded… tired, torn, and wondering how I'd ever get Nick out of my heart and mind.

We filled the rest of our time with fun banter, good food, shared stories, and plans for the future. I couldn't help but laugh at seeing Abby go on and on about how excited she was to spread her wings and explore a new place with the love of her life, even while a dark cloud hung over her parents' heads since they obviously hated the fact that she was going away.

Seeing Abby so secure in her choices gave me more to think about. The distance didn't help the turmoil within my heart, but being away from Nick helped me see the situation between me, Mike, and Nick from a different perspective.

Everything Nick had said over the last few days was on constant replay. My body craved his touch and my heart hurt from the distance between us. I didn't know if I was ever going to see him again, but Abby was right. I had never felt this way about Mike.

In the end, I concluded that I should let Mike go. Then he could find someone who would love him the way he deserved to be loved. And that person wasn't me.

That night, I slept well for the first time in a very long time.

Chapter 19

By the time Monday evening rolled around, we had finished eating dinner with Abby's family and said our goodbyes before heading to Boston.

We pulled out of the driveway and she sent a message on our group chat.

Heading to the Scottish Pub. Anyone in?

Summer break had officially started at our university. Most of our friends had already left the city, and those who were staying took odd jobs and worked weird hours. It was hard to gauge how many of them would actually show up.

Messages started popping up on Abby's phone. Apparently, more of them had no plans for the evening than we'd thought. Excited about the fun evening ahead, we blasted music and sang along during the entire drive back to Boston.

____

At a quarter past nine, we entered the Scottish Pub. My heart sank the moment I saw Mike. Along with Abby's boyfriend,

Parker, and the rest of the gang, Mike was at the bar ordering cheese fries.

Abby must've sensed my unease. "There is no deadline here. Do what makes you happy," she whispered in my ear as we made our way to the table.

I nodded, but in reality, I had already made my decision. Executing it would be an entirely different story.

"Have you checked your phone lately?" Abby asked before we reached our table. I shook my head. It wasn't Abby's fault, but she didn't get it. I had been there before, waiting for Nick for days that turned into months and years. I couldn't let history repeat itself.

The music was loud, the atmosphere was boisterous. Abby sat down next to Parker and gave him a kiss. I said hi to everyone and sat as far away from Mike as possible. It didn't take long before everyone noticed the awkwardness and started giving each other quizzical looks.

Thankfully, they kept their questions to themselves.

Mike and I exchanged cordial smiles. Neither one of us made any effort to talk to each other. In his jeans and sky-blue T-shirt, he seemed to be in his element. Maybe he was surprised to see me here, but he didn't make his feelings known.

We ordered beers for the table. Lucky for me, the alcohol helped to disperse the tension and we all fell into easy conversations, discussing how relieved we were that the finals were behind us and what we were going to do over the summer break.

By eleven, Mike decided to call it a night. Everyone at the table booed him. "I had a long day," he tried to explain. His words caused more booing.

Mike stood up. The next thing I knew, he was standing beside me and asking me to walk him out. Not wanting to make this even weirder than it already was, I left my drink and purse on the table and followed him outside.

The air conditioner inside was out of control, which was why the air outside felt so much warmer. We waited until our ears got adjusted to the quiet. "When did you come back to Boston?" I asked.

"Around ten and went straight to work."

"Ah, that makes sense. It really has been a long day for you, then."

"Yeah. I had to get up at five to help Dad with some electrical issues in the house."

"Did you fix it?"

"I got it working before I had to leave. Just because I study physics, my dad expects me to fix all the broken things in the house."

That got a chuckle out of me because it was true. No one called him as often as his dad did, and those calls often resulted in drives up to their family home.

We kept the conversation going. It was stunted. I wouldn't be surprised if Mike felt it, too.

"It's good to see you here, back in your element," Mike decided to address the elephant in the room. "This is the Ivy I know. The girl I met on Saturday... she was someone else altogether."

I took a second to digest his words. "And you think *this* is the real me?"

"I guess I should ask you that. Sometimes we feel we know a person well enough until they turn out to be someone else entirely." He exhaled loudly, as though a weight had lifted when he started talking to me. "Honestly, I didn't know you were rich."

Ignoring his comment about my wealth, mostly because I couldn't justify why I was keeping it a secret from him, I concentrated on the rest. "Did I really seem that different?"

"You were different enough to make me wonder which one is the real you." He stated his observation without sugarcoating a thing. "But I get it. You didn't want to be completely honest with me because you probably didn't think this would last. I'm not rich, so I don't fit your criteria or whatever."

I shook my head. "Having money was not, is not, and will never be a factor in me choosing who I spend my life with. I'm not that superficial."

Or am I?

The uncomfortable silence stretched and stretched until I finally gathered enough strength to speak again. "You asked us to step out and talk. I'm listening."

"I want to go back to the discussion we had at Ryan's engagement party. After what happened, I don't think we should rush into moving in together."

I wasn't sure if I felt elated or sad that we had both reached the same conclusion, but I definitely felt relieved. "That's a good idea."

"I always knew something was holding you back," Mike continued. "Somehow, I thought you might be ready now that undergrad is over. But now I understand that classes, and us being young, had nothing to do with it."

"I'm not sure what you're getting at."

"We've been together for two years. But I never felt like you committed to this relationship the way I committed myself to it. You'd always find excuses not to meet my family. You never wanted to stay over. Your agreement to move in honestly shocked me."

"I was busy and you were, too. And don't make it seem like I never spent time with you because that's not true." I tried defending myself, but it was the nagging feeling that he was right that overwhelmed me.

"Remember those awful snowstorms? I stayed over at your place. You slept on the couch because you got a running injury and sleeping there was supposedly better for your back? And all the times that we stayed up late to study, even when we finished work in the middle of the night, and you would run back to your apartment instead of staying with me?"

The complaints started pouring out of him. Did these things just dawn on him, or had they been on his mind for a while? Either way, his genuine frustration and obvious pain left me speechless. Telling him about my adultery burned on the tip of my tongue.

"Was going to Abby's house more important than spending time with me and seeing my family? Did you even realize how many times my parents came here to meet you and you came up with some stupid excuse to get out of it? I had let everything slide, but I can't do it anymore. It ends here."

I had no response to any of his accusations. There was only one thing left to do.

"I couldn't be the girlfriend you deserve, Mike." My eyes stung. "I'm so sorry. I truly am." That was all I could manage because that much was true.

He was holding onto the hope that I would tell him we were on the same page. That I loved him the way he loved me. But I couldn't lie. Not to Mike, and not to myself.

"Mike." A tear trickled down my eyes. "I'm sorry, I can't do this anymore, either. I want to break up."

Hurt, rejection, sorrow… I saw all of these emotions flash in his eyes before he turned around and walked away. I couldn't get myself to confess I cheated on him. Couldn't let him lose faith from love.

Chapter 20

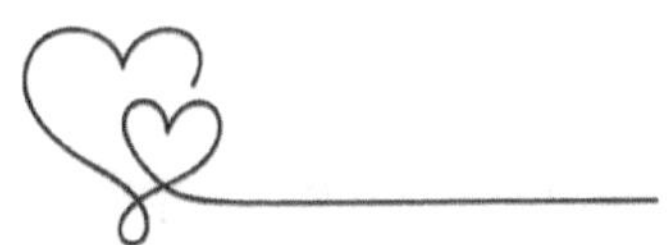

An aching pain started rolling through my chest. I still hoped it was my imagination, that I was going to wake up soon and the last ninety-six hours would be nothing more than scenes from yet another one of my vivid dreams that appeared all too real.

I tried to be happy with what I had, but Nick consumed my every thought. We hadn't met in years, I had intentionally stayed as far away from him as possible, and yet I couldn't break through the spell he had put on me.

A bell chimed when I pulled the door handle to go back inside the pub, but the sound triggered something and I changed my mind. I turned around and started walking toward my apartment.

A few blocks later, I changed my mind again and walked the opposite way.

I should've been sad about what had happened between Mike and me. The time I spent with Nick wasn't even a fraction of the time I had spent with Mike, and yet it felt like someone had cut out my heart because I missed Nick so much.

He had monopolized every inch of my heart from as far back as I could remember.

No matter how much time I spent with someone, a day with Nick could destroy every other relationship I ever had. Abby told me to go find love and live my life, but my life started and ended with only one man—Nick.

These emotional reflections started tiring me out. I gave up on walking aimlessly and headed home.

As soon as I got to my building, I stuck my hand into my pocket and the realization hit me. My apartment keys and fob to enter the building weren't there.

How can they be when you left them at the bar?

I knocked on the glass door of the building, hoping that Jose, the security guard who covered the night-shift, would hear me and let me in. It was Ryan who insisted that I live in an apartment with twenty-four-seven security guards on the premises. Abby and I didn't care about that, but it was a battle we couldn't win. Eventually we had moved in here and since Ryan owned the building, we got to stay rent free and that helped Abby save some money.

Jose came to the door to open it right away. "Miss Ivy, hi! Coming back from another late-night run?"

"Something like that," I said. "It's a long story, but I don't have my keys or my fob on me. Do you have a copy?"

"I do, but you can go right up. Miss Abby and her guests are home. They seemed worried."

I had left all of my things at the bar and had not come back after my conversation with Mike. It was also late and dark. It was also not the first time I had done that.

I was about to ask who Abby's guests were when the desk phone rang, a jarring sound at this time of the night that filled the lobby. Jose headed to his desk and I walked over to the elevator, dreaming about a shower, eating my feelings while watching some trashy reality TV show, and going to bed.

Lost in thought about how Mike might've been healing his own wound and how I hated myself for hurting him, I pressed the button for the seventh floor.

The elevator shook a little as it ascended, as it usually did. The door opened at its designated floor, and I headed for the apartment at the end of the hallway.

My apartment door flew open even before I reached it… and standing in front of me was the person I least expected to see tonight.

Nick's gaze burned hot. His eyes were bloodshot, his hair was disheveled, and he had a day's worth of stubble on his face. He looked awful, or at least as awful as a sizzling-hot man could ever look.

For as long as I had known Nick, I'd never seen him like this before. But that wasn't even the weirdest part. What was he doing in Boston and why was he in my apartment?

"Are you all right?" he asked, sounding a little breathless.

"Of course."

He stepped aside and let me walk into my apartment. Abby stood there with her arms crossed and a look of horror etched into her features. "What is wrong with you? Why did you leave without your phone? No, why leave in the first place without saying anything?"

Parker was sitting on the couch, seemingly eager to hear what I had to say, too.

Puzzled, my eyes darted between Abby and Parker. Apparently, my disappearing act had scared more people than I realized.

"Mike wanted to talk to me and then I went for a walk."

Abby came closer. "How many times did I tell you to check your phone?" She scoffed and nodded towards Nick, who was now leaning against the wall. His concern was gone, but his angry demeanor was seemingly unchanged.

Abby walked over to Parker and motioned for him to get up. "I'll spend the night at Parker's so you two can have some privacy and talk," she said. "Your phone was dead. I put it on the kitchen charger. Call me if you need me."

Once Abby and Parker walked out, Nick locked the door and resumed the same position by the door. His eyes hadn't left me since I entered the apartment.

"What are you doing here, Nick?" I asked, sounding as tired as I felt.

If he wanted to kill me with his silence, it was working. Too nervous to stay still and be stared at, I went to the pantry, grabbed two bottles of water, and offered Nick one—only to be met with more silence.

I leaned back against the fridge, mirroring him and keeping as much distance between us as the space allowed. "Will you really not say anything?"

"Do you have any idea how infuriating you are?"

The man finally speaks, and he says this?

"Excuse me?"

He was in my town. In my house. He was the one not explaining why he was here, and *I* was the infuriating person?

He threw his next question at me. "Did you break up with Mike?"

"Why would that matter to you?"

"I'm not in the mood to play games, Ivy. I need to know if you're together or not."

Now it was my turn to say nothing. Served him right.

He walked over to the couch and sat down like he owned the place. I leaned against the island, still maintaining the same amount of distance from him and pretending I was in control of the situation.

I certainly wasn't.

"Can we talk like adults? Tell me if you broke up with Mike." Quickly, he started rubbing me the wrong way. "And don't tell me you're in love with him. That pathetic kiss at Ryan's party was laughable, to say the least. You can try fooling Mike with that, but you can't fool me."

The anger and frustration that had been building inside of me suddenly had no place to go. Before I could stop myself, I took the water bottle that I had set down on the kitchen island and threw it at Nick with full force. He ducked. We both watched the bottle hit the glass doors of the balcony, fall to the floor with a loud thud, and roll under the couch.

"Are you out of your mind?"

I crossed my arms over my chest, hugging myself. "Hmm. Maybe I am. How about we talk about you for a change? Have you broken up with *your* Mindy?" I asked, mimicking him.

He laughed, which stirred up my anger even more. "*You* are mine. Mindy is just... Mindy."

"That's not what I asked."

We both kept staring at each other, challenging each other.

"Yes, we're done. She's been taken care of."

"What does that mean?" I asked, but then shook my head. "No. You know what? I don't want to hear it. All I know is that I never want to see her ever again."

"Consider it done." The impact of his words momentarily halted my train of thought. I didn't mean it in a literal sense; I just wanted to vex him like he did me. Nick continued, "Unlike you, I take care of my problems rather than running away from them."

I glared at him. "I came home. I didn't run away."

He eased back on the couch and patted the spot next to him. "Would you mind?"

"Thank you. I'm fine where I am."

His eyes darkened. I had a feeling he wasn't used to people not giving in to his demands.

"Okay. So I drop you off at your home and you run. You didn't share your number and I didn't want to get Ryan worried on his vacation. So, I jumped through hoops to get it, only to realize that you don't pick up people's calls." He was as close to being livid as I had ever seen him. "I put my work on hold to come here and talk to you in person. But when I get here, you're nowhere to be found. Finally I find your roommate and she tells me you went to the bar together, but then you took off without your phone, your wallet, or your keys. Now tell me, Ivy. If you're not infuriating, then what are you?"

I chose not to respond.

Nick didn't budge.

A ball of hurt and guilt rose in my chest as the minutes ticked away. It very much felt like we were playing a game of *Who Will Break First?*

Unfortunately, I lost. "First of all, I didn't run," I clarified again. "I thought we were done. I had no idea you would follow me here or that you wanted to speak to me at all. You never asked me for my number. And even if you had asked, my phone died on Saturday night." As I explained, I simultaneously counted the answers to his stupid question on my fingers.

He stayed quiet, as though he was replaying my answers in his head. "When did I say we were done?"

Flustered by the tension that filled the apartment, I walked over to the pantry and found another bottle of water. This time I intended to drink from it rather than aim it at Nick's head. "This feels more like an interrogation than a discussion," I told him. "Do you think you can come here and scold me like I'm a child because things didn't go the way you wanted them to go?"

"If you claim to be a mature adult, then why are you constantly running?"

"*I'm* running?" I yelled. "*You're* the one who took off!"

"I had to go to work."

"What work? I made that shit up so Ryan wouldn't get suspicious," I reminded him.

"Sweetheart, my life doesn't revolve around you," he mocked. "People actually work in real life."

"Only assassins and mafias work so late in the night."

His gaze hardened, but whatever he was going to say, he reined it in. "You seem to have forgotten the conversation we had that night." He chose to go back to our original conversation. "How convenient."

"No, Nick. I didn't forget anything. You made your stance abundantly clear and I did, too. I won't leave Boston and you can't leave Manhattan. End of story. Now, are we done?"

"Hardly." He got up and moved forward with determination. The more steps he took, the more I backed away.

My body responded to him in the worst possible way, as if I had forgotten all the suffering endured in the last couple of days. Like I wanted to be drawn back into his vortex.

Sexual tension brewing and thickening, he erased the last few feet that remained between us without breaking our eye contact. My heartbeat pounded in my ears as he caged me between his arms, bent down, and touched me with his lips.

I tried to move away before my brain could fully short-circuit. Between the island and his arms, I had little room to wiggle. "I can't," I mumbled.

"You can't, or you won't? Because our bodies react the same way whenever we're around each other. I can feel it and so do you."

"I can't do this," I repeated.

He wrapped his powerful arms around and dragged me further into him. "Give me a good reason."

I tried again to push him away, ignoring my body's insistence on surrendering.

"Don't walk away, Ivy. It's not helping."

"You being near me isn't helping either, Nick. I can't think straight around you."

"And you think I can? You've ruined me even without being in my life. I couldn't be with anyone, couldn't have any meaningful relationship because of you. You weren't even around, and yet not a day went by without me thinking about you. What else can I say for you to understand that I can't live without you?"

His confession left me in shock, but my doubts wouldn't let me live this moment. "You know this would never work."

He cupped my face and tilted my head back. "Start by putting an end to constantly running away," he breathed. "We can figure out the rest."

With a chaste kiss, he released my face, took my hand, and led me to the couch.

"I'm serious, Ivy," he said, once he sat down opposite from me. "I want you in my life. Our chemistry is unlike anything I have ever felt before—that's already established. But I want to know you. I want to know what you like to eat, what kind of music you like, what scares you, and what makes you happy. That's not possible until we're living in the same city."

Bending over, he put his elbow over his legs and took my hand in his. "Tell me what you need me to do, so we can find a middle ground. We've waited far too long. Now that we're here, I can't lose you again."

He was saying all the right things. Everything that I'd always wanted to hear. But I couldn't process it until he answered a question that had been burning a hole through my heart. "Why now?" I asked.

"Like I said, we've wasted so much time already. There's no point in wasting any more on meaningless fucks when all we want is each other," he said. "I was upset when you joined Harvard instead of coming home. By the time I came to my senses and was ready to tell you how I felt, you were already introducing Mike to Ryan."

"And what changed now?"

"Your return was an overwhelming force that reminded me I'm still crazy about you and I still want you. We're still in a tough spot with you being Ryan's sister and all, but even with all the obstacles in the way I want you more than I've ever wanted anyone."

"This is a big deal for me. If I give in and move for you, my entire life will change. And what happens if you get bored of me? I'll be the one who'll have to rebuild my life from scratch."

"Do you seriously think I can get bored of you? If that was possible, what are we doing here after all these years?"

"I don't know, Nick. You tell me."

Exhaling, he brought my hand closer to his chest and put it right over his heart. "All I ask is for you to take a leap of faith and move back to New York. Like I said, there's nothing in Boston that you can't do there. Even your professor is there now. I don't see why it'd be so hard to at least give it a try."

"You're asking for a lot."

"I am. And I want you to trust me and jump with me. How else will we figure out how to make this relationship work unless we do it together?"

He had valid points. "And if I say no?"

He inhaled deeply. I couldn't let go. "I want you, Ivy, anyway I can have you. If you don't want to move, we'll figure out something else; but this can't be the end of the road for us."

"I want you too," I admitted, then bit my bottom lip. "So, what category of *fuck* does our night at the beach fall under?"

Impishly, he tugged me into his lap. His heated gaze met mine as I trembled in his arms. His lips claimed my mouth and my body instantly surrendered.

"I don't have words to define what we did that night, sweetheart, but it surely wasn't a fuck."

I kissed him, simultaneously running my fingers through his hair. "Find the words. I want to hear it," I whispered.

Nick let out a low growl. "Okay. It was a life-altering moment that left no doubt in my mind we are meant to be together."

Unable to hold back the tears that were threatening to spill out, I pulled away. "Then why did you leave in such a hurry after you dropped me off at Ryan's? It really hurt me. One minute we're having an argument and the next minute you're gone. I thought you wanted to wash your hands of me as soon as we had sex."

Realizing his mistake, he shut his eyes and shook his head. "I would never do that. I left because I had to sort out a work thing. That's the truth. By the time I returned to Ryan's apartment, you were gone." He caressed my cheek. "I want all of you, Ivy, not just your body. This physical chemistry is not the only thing between us. We share something a lot more profound and deep down you know it, too."

"Show me like you mean it." It wasn't a request. I really wanted to know.

Holding my nape, his lips claimed mine. All the pain I had felt suddenly seemed insignificant compared to my feelings for him. I wanted Nick more than my next breath. Our pasts were threads woven together, and our fates intertwined since the dawn of time.

This night wasn't for sleeping. It was for exploring each other. We made love. Again. And again. Fast and slow. We toured every curve and every bend of each other. I ran my fingers up and down his muscles while his mouth tasted every inch of me, memorizing me, learning all of my pleasure points, and whispering flowery words in my ear.

Chapter 21

I woke up to the sound of my muffled ringtone. The clock on my dresser didn't matter; it just reminded me I had overslept. It was approaching seven in the morning.

Nick's soft breath tickled my neck. His arms were wrapped around my chest and our feet were a tangled closeness. My body hummed from being so near him. My heart fluttered as my dream became a reality.

My cell phone rang again, the sound making Nick stir. I turned around and kissed his cheek. "It's my phone in the kitchen. I'll go turn it off."

He groaned. Without opening his eyes, he pulled me under him and started placing featherlike kisses along my neck. His rough stubble teased my skin. I reacted instantly.

My phone rang again.

"I should probably get that. It might be important."

Reluctantly, he rolled off of me. "Don't take too long. We have unfinished business."

I giggled, kissed him on the cheek, and raced to the kitchen. My phone was where Abby had left it—placed on the charger on the kitchen counter.

Now that my phone was charged, I saw all the notifications I had missed. There were over fifty missed calls from an unknown number, twenty messages from that same number, and a text message from Ryan.

Before I could read further, my phone started ringing again. "Abby?"

"Where were you? I've been trying to reach you since six!"

"Hey! Sorry, my phone was in the kitchen. It took me a minute to get to it."

"Or an hour," she complained. Hearing my voice, though, she relaxed and turned frisky. *"Does that mean you two… how should I say it… made up?"*

"Yeah, we made up." I smiled irrevocably. "Let's just say it was the best night of my life."

"Is that excitement I hear? Finally!"

I couldn't stop laughing. Abby joined in. Holding the phone between my neck and my shoulder, I poured water into the coffeemaker.

"I'm heading to work directly from Parker's," Abby said. *"Will I see you this evening?"*

"Yeah. I'll be home."

We spoke some more until the coffee machine warmed up and made a noise. Once I hung up, I prepared two cups of dark roast coffee and tiptoed to my bedroom.

Nick was sitting up and leaning back on the tall headboard with my white pillow tucked behind his back. The Egyptian white cotton sheet covered the most decadent parts of his nakedness. He had such a dominating presence that my room, unable to contain it all, seemed to have shrunk.

"Black, no sugar. Not sure how you like it." I handed Nick his coffee.

"That works." He placed the mug on the nightstand next to him. "Come here."

His eyes, now soft and filled with love, confirmed that the night had been as satisfying for him as it was for me. Putting my coffee cup next to his, I climbed into bed and sat down beside him. Unable to keep the distance, he wrapped his hands around me and showered me with kisses. Drunk on love, I snuggled into the crook of his neck, needing this proximity more than I needed air to breathe.

"Can't believe I'm saying this, but I have to go to work today. I neglected all my meetings these last few days and things are piling up."

"Of course. I understand. What time is your flight?" Being the CEO of a multi-billion-dollar company, he surely had a lot of people relying on his input.

"Not flying to New York just yet. I'll work out of my Boston office."

My heart skipped with joy. "Sounds good to me," I chirped.

"It better." He smiled. "If only I had known how much one night of work would cost me."

"Smartass."

"I don't want you to pull a stunt like that ever again. I'm not Ryan."

Seriously? I arched my brow. "Don't tell me what to do. I'm not Mindy."

He pursed his lips. Assessing me before responding. "I like to have control over things. I'd rather give you a heads-up now, so the expectations are set."

"Lower your expectations then, because you can't control me."

"Not control you," Nick corrected. "Take care of you."

"Well, now that you put it like that… not that I need it, but it's something I'm okay with."

"You sure are something else." He chuckled and gave me a kiss. "I'm staying at the Ritz. Can we meet for dinner tonight?"

"I was going to see Abby in the evening, but I can work something out."

"Can you do eight?"

"I'll make it work!" I said excitedly.

"There's one more thing." He repositioned me so that I straddled him. I would've been self-conscious around Mike, but with Nick, I embraced my nakedness. "I have to be in New York tomorrow morning. My charter leaves at six. Can we go together? And before you say no, technically you're on vacation this week."

I bent down and kissed his chin. "Since you asked me nicely, I will think about it."

Nick gently kissed my forehead, and then got up and stood at the foot of the bed. I thought he was going to drink his coffee instead; he started kissing my leg. Starting from my ankle where my scar was, he moved up to my thigh, and then to my hip bone, and then to my back. His firm hands squeezed my butt cheeks before they started trailing up my waist. I gasped as he pulled me to the edge of the bed, flipped me over, and started kissing my belly.

"You're so greedy," I stated, squirming under his touch.

"It's your fault. You're too damn enticing."

"I thought you had work to do?"

"Work has to wait."

After last night, I didn't think my body could handle another orgasm; but I was aroused, slick, and ready to go again. Bending down, he went missionary. His tall frame covered me completely. His thick erection nudged my labia, tempting me once again. Soon, his slick, hard shaft started moving inside of me. Sparks radiated from every cell, sending wild tremors to my core.

He groaned. Going slowly, he nudged a bundle of nerves every time he moved. I inhaled his scent: bergamot and Nick mixed with sex. It was divine.

"Remember this feeling next time your feet are itching to run away from me."

And he continued. In and out, in and out, in an even rhythm. "Do you feel this, sweetheart?"

I moaned in pleasure, unable to form a word, let alone express my feelings in that moment.

"It's... us. You and me..." Nick's whispered words filled my ears and then traveled to my heart.

My core rippled under his touch. My sex clenched around him and he knew exactly what to do because, a few strokes later, I shuddered as massive, satisfying spasms came over my entire body. He joined me and let out a low, guttural growl that was music to my ears.

As our eyes locked, still basking in the afterglow of pleasure, I saw in his gaze the love I had always yearned for. It simmered brightly, reflecting the depth of our connection. Happiness and contentment. Love and gratification.

With a chaste kiss on my forehead, he rose to his feet. Drained and utterly sated, I succumbed to the deepest, most delicious sleep. My soul separated from my physical body and, as I looked upon myself, I watched my face aglow with unmistakable bliss.

At some point, Nick woke me up with a kiss on my forehead.

I opened my eyes and smiled at his freshly showered face.

"I won't be able to go to work at all if you keep looking this cute when you sleep," he teased, a smile dancing on the corner of his lips. There was that dimple again that drove me crazy.

"Is it okay that you're going to work in yesterday's clothes? Unshaved? Won't anyone notice?" I yawned and watched him put on his wrinkled white shirt.

"Perks of being a boss, I can do whatever I want. Besides, I'll change in my office. I've everything I need there."

Nick turned around and gave me a full view of his gorgeous physique. My heart stopped beating. Regardless of the time we spent together, I felt drawn to him. And to his taut body.

My bed caved in slightly when he sat down next to me. He pulled the sheet to cover me, probably so he wouldn't get distracted again.

"You're such a tease." He moved a few rogue strands of hair away from my face. "Just so you're clear, we are not done."

He waited for my nod, confirming that I heard him loud and clear.

He took my hand and gently kissed my knuckles. "We're in uncharted territory and we both don't know how to navigate around each other yet. Will figure it out though, together. Just tell me one thing."

I looked into his deep emerald eyes.

"Are you in?" His gaze searched for an answer. "Say it, Ivy. I need to hear it."

Although I had no control over myself as far as Nick was concerned, there was only one answer I could give him.

"I'm all in."

Chapter 22

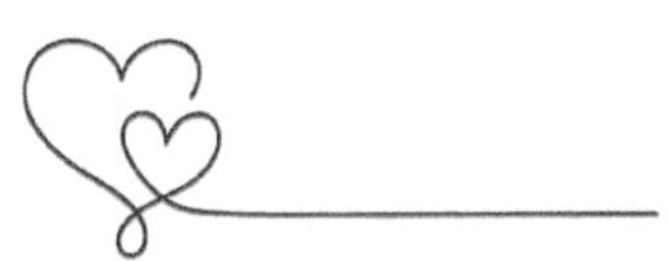

After taking a long shower, I went to the living room and made the executive decision to prepare a few moving boxes. I labeled them *Abby, Ivy*, and *Trash*, and put a fresh roll of packing tape on the coffee table. If I left it up to Abby, she wouldn't pack until she drove off. And since I put her in a terrible situation last night, it was my solemn responsibility to make up for it by giving her a hand.

Although I wasn't sure where I was going to live in a few weeks, one thing was certain. It was time to pack my things and see where life would take me next.

For the next couple of hours, I concentrated on the work before me and packed fifteen boxes. I decided not to close them, in case Abby wanted to go through them first.

By the time the clock struck five thirty, I was pretty satisfied with how much I had accomplished. Sweaty from all the bending and running around I had done, I took another shower and headed back into my bedroom.

I didn't know why it happened at that precise moment, but I suddenly recalled Rosanne's words about my mother's wishes for me to stay connected to my roots and how much Ryan missed having me around. Standing in this nearly empty apartment, it was time for me to look ahead and consider my present and my future.

For the first time, the haze lifted. I started seeing my future with some clarity and could think about what it would be like to go back home.

After changing into a cotton sundress, I settled down on the balcony with my phone in my hand.

Thankfully, only a few new notifications had popped up since the morning. First was a day-old message from Ryan.

You forgot your brother already? Just wanted to make sure you're enjoying your stay in the city. BTW, I got a delivery notification. Since no one was home, they left the package with Doug at the front office. Good to know you're partying all night and sleeping all day. Keep it up.

Followed by heart and kiss emojis.

I read the message and realized he didn't know I wasn't in New York. My new mantra would be *to keep people in the loop.*

I typed a quick response.

Sorry. I came back to Boston. Will head back soon. Love you. Say hi to Risha for me.

I added a few *love-you* and *missing-you* GIFs as well, so he knew everything was okay.

The next message was from Dustin.

Hi stranger, I thought we were going to meet, but I haven't heard from you since MoxTo. Let me know if Thursday evening works for you. Noah and Rach are free and would love to join.

I sat up in my chair with excitement. It had been ages since I'd seen them.

Sorry, I've been busy. Thursday works. Can't wait to see you all.

Another new message popped up on my phone at that very second, only this one was from an unknown number.

Do you ever check your phone?

After going through all the messages from this number, I understood who it was.

Nick?

Immediately, dots appear on the screen.

Albeit. Who else is texting you?

I laughed. **Too many boyfriends to keep track. I get confused.**

I hope it's a joke.

What's with him and his sense of humor? **Tell me what you want.**

So now I need a reason to message you? And you still haven't answered my question.

I loved seeing him jealous, but after everything we just went through, I didn't want to get him worked up for no reason.

You don't. And it was a joke. I miss you.

She finally says what I want to hear. Can't wait to see you.

My smile turned into a wide grin. **Same here.**

You still haven't given me a clear answer about the Mike situation.

Hurting Mike's feelings wasn't something I was ready to talk about. I kept typing and deleting until his next message popped up.

Made a reservation at Mentosina. Unfortunately, I have meetings until seven-thirty. My driver will pick you up at a quarter after seven.

Nick, I have a car and a driver's license. I'm more than capable of driving myself to the restaurant.

The dots kept showing up and disappearing for some time before a new text popped up. *Don't fight me on this. See you at eight.*

Fine. See you then. Can't wait!

I soaked in the mesmerizing beauty of Fresh Pond Reservoir—a stunning view of the most beautiful park in Boston. My balcony was undoubtedly the best feature of this apartment.

The early evening breeze carried a faint scent of the reservoir water, caressing my face and playing with my hair. From my vantage point, blue water shimmered under the setting sun, reflecting the sky and the patches of white clouds.

I had lost count of how many laps I'd done around this park, but I loved every inch of the trail. I was not sure what it was going to be like to not run there every day. My routine for the last four years was going to change.

Closing my eyes, I inhaled deeply and took in all the familiar scents. Tranquil and inviting, it was my peaceful solitude amid the bustle. Boston had become my home, but had my relationship with the city run its course?

Fear drove my mind wild. My thoughts jumped between my two worlds. In this world, everything was in order. A peaceful cocoon that was missing one important piece—my heart—which was now with a man I was getting to know again. The second world was new and chaotic, where I'd have to start my life all over again and where I didn't know what the future held. My heart lived there.

Then there were the reasons I had run away. My haunted past. The thousands of fears that plagued me. Was I ready to take that leap of faith? Could I do it if it meant getting to be with Nick?

A sudden squeal from inside the apartment made me jump. I turned, knowing too well my best friend was home.

"Girl, Nick is seriously hot and *way* intense in person!" Abby squealed excitedly as soon as she stepped onto the balcony. "And, hello, it's Nicholas freaking Branson, currently the most eligible bachelor in the country!"

I couldn't stop laughing. I never thought of him as Nicholas Branson, the CEO of Branson Capital, and someone every woman in America wanted to marry. To me, he was just Nick, a guy who loved riding his bike and playing soccer every chance he got. He was the only man who I could share all my joys and sorrows with without worrying about being judged.

Abby gave me a full rundown from the time she met Nick until I walked through the door. "After going through all the security cameras in Manhattan—he must be pretty powerful to do something like that, by the way—he found out that you took the train to Boston. What he didn't know is that you took another train to Marlborough. You really made him run around in circles trying to find you, Ivy. And poor Jose—Nick made his life absolute hell until you walked into the building."

No wonder he was so angry when I saw him last night. I didn't make it easy trying to locate me for two full days.

"Even though I told him at least a dozen times that it's very normal for you to come up with plans on the fly, he was a nervous wreck until he saw you."

"I wasn't expecting him to do all that. Nick never came after me the last time I left. That time I waited, I cried, and I eventually moved on. He still didn't show up."

"I don't know what changed. But he doesn't seem to play around like you said he had done before, I can tell you that much."

When she looked inside the apartment, she noticed all the boxes I had prepared. In her excitement earlier, she completely missed all the work I had done. "You rock! What am I going to do in Cali without you?"

"Miss me like crazy?"

"Obviously."

She hugged me like only a best friend could. "Okay listen," I said once we broke apart. "I didn't close the boxes in case you wanted to go through them. But, let me remind you there's another beast we have to tackle here."

Abby raised an eyebrow.

"We need to sell the furniture. I'm sure you're not planning to lug it all to the West Coast with you."

"Yup. We're definitely selling it all."

We sidelined our discussion on Nick and spent the next thirty minutes laughing and joking as we moved from room to room, reminiscing about how and why we had picked out these pieces of furniture, and looking at what kind of work we had ahead of us.

We were excited that the undergrad was behind us and that we were about to start the next chapter of our lives; but leaving what had been our home base for the past two years was bittersweet. All the times we had shared, and all the laughs we had had, would be nothing but memories. No matter how much I tried not to make this an emotional parting, I would be sad and lonely once Abby left.

Even though I came from money, I never threw my money around because I never wanted to make people uncomfortable. I lived a modest life in Boston. We shared everything in half. I never bought anything extravagant if Abby couldn't afford it. My clothes and shoes were the only exception I splurged on. After all, I grew up reading Vogue and shopping with Mrs. Sandra McAlister, who thought underdressing was a crime.

"Wait! Aren't you planning to take any of the furniture? Especially the Adirondack chairs you fought with me about and finally bought?"

I chuckled. I had spent an entire week trying with everything in my power to convince her that we needed those chairs for our balcony. In the end, I won, but it wasn't an easy battle.

"I won't need them," I told her. "Mike and I are not moving in together."

"That's wonderful news!" she said and meant it. Not that she didn't like Mike, but we had never had a strong bond and Abby could see right through me.

"Aren't you surprised, though?"

"To be honest, I am. I mean, I know I always give the right advice. But I've never seen you taking anyone's advice before."

I pulled back in surprise. "What are you talking about? I always listen to you."

"Sure." She rolled her eyes. "Of course you listen, but then you do what you want to do in the end. I'm glad this time around you did what I suggested you should do."

I told her all about my breakup with Mike and filled her in on my discussion with Nick. By the time I was done, we were back on the balcony.

"What do you want, Ivy? Why are you not considering moving back to New York? I mean, seriously: What is holding you back?"

"I have always wanted to be with Nick," I said, more to myself than to Abby.

"In that case, what's stopping you from taking a risk? Your heart is with him anyway, and that man was in a literal panic until he saw you. He has genuine feelings for you, Ivy. Those kinds of feelings don't develop overnight. Not being able to reach you, that fear of losing you—he wasn't faking it. Did you know he had an entire team out looking for you?"

"A team? You're joking, right?"

"I am not. He seriously thought he'd lost you. From the time we walked into the building and for the next few hours after that, he tried to figure out how to get to you. Never once did he ask me if you spoke to me about him, or what your feelings were for him. Even though he somehow figured out that we are best friends, his only focus was finding you and making sure you were safe."

Stunned, I took it all in.

"I've deep feelings for him, I won't deny that, but I have my doubts too. I don't know what it's like being part of that world anymore. It's a major lifestyle change."

"Nothing in life is easy, Ivy. You know that better than anyone. But if you don't give something a chance, how will you know if it will work? You both like each other, so why don't you think it's worth giving the relationship a shot?"

"I don't know, Abby." Every bone in my body agreed with her. I wanted Nick so bad. Yet, I stood undecided.

"You lost your parents. That kind of loss is hard to deal with and it can traumatize a person for life. Are you scared that you're going to lose Nick, too, so you're choosing to let him go before that can even happen?"

"I got over that fear a long time ago," I affirmed to her. "It's the unknown that worries me. And then I wonder if I should go back to my roots—to my home and to Nick—because that's where I belong."

I turned to my side to look at the glimmering, golden reflection of the sky on the surface of the pond. No matter how many times I had seen that sunset from my balcony, it never failed to take my breath away.

Nick was right when he told me we'd never grasp the true essence of our feelings for each other until we gave our relationship a shot. For that to happen, we had to be closer to each other. Undoubtedly, it would be a big change, especially for me; but I wanted Nick to the point of insanity and he wanted me too. He had told me that and showed it to me many, many times. If I moved to Manhattan, I would also get to spend more time with Ryan and Risha—not to mention being able to attend Professor Sinclair's classes.

It was frightening and exhilarating at the same time.

"How do you think Ryan would react to you and Nick being together?" Abby asked, pulling me out of my thoughts.

"Honestly? I have no idea. They're best friends and all, but it could go either way." A queasy sensation filled my stomach. "It's just another thing I would have to work through before making any big decisions, I guess."

If I moved, I'd be jumping without a safety net. In the end, it could be the best thing I had ever done in my life. Or it could be the worst thing imaginable. But in order to find out, I would have to let go and jump.

Chapter 23

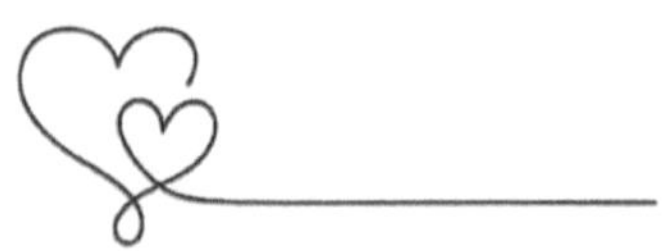

I had lost track of time. Leaving Abby, I ran to my bedroom to change.

I scrimmaged through my closet until I found the perfect outfit for tonight: a new pair of low-rise skinny jeans that I hadn't worn yet; a rose gold corset that pushed up my breasts and put my stomach on full display; and an emerald green Kate Spade blazer, so I could take it off and watch Nick's eyes fill with lust.

Throwing on a pair of matching green stilettos, putting my hair up in a ponytail, and applying some nude lip gloss onto my lips, I was ready to impress him.

I waved to Abby, who was still on the balcony and, from the sound of it, talking to her property manager in SoCal. Then I rushed downstairs to where a car was already waiting for me.

"She's with me."

I heard Nick's voice behind me as soon as I entered the restaurant and the maître d' asked for my name. I turned quickly, and the air around us crackled immediately.

Nick put his hand on the small of my back. My voice caught in my throat when I saw his beautiful, chiseled face. Masculinity and sophistication were wrapped up together in a perfectly ironed white shirt, a gray pinstripe vest, and a tie that accentuated the color of his eyes. The jacket was gone and his shirt sleeve was folded back enough to show the hues of gold on his arms.

He was the most gorgeous man I had ever seen, and he was all mine.

"You look stunning," he said, firm and loud, not caring for the people around us.

"Mr. Branson, your table is ready," the maître d' said; but even as we started walking, Nick's eyes remained trained on me.

"The corset looks good. But I would rather see you without it," he whispered in my ear.

"Nick!" I whispered right back, the heat pooling in my cheeks. "You can't say stuff like that in public. In case you haven't noticed, everyone is watching us." Literally.

"Well, sweetheart, get used to it. This is just the beginning." With a wide grin on his face, he pulled the chair out for me and then took a seat opposite mine. As if finally realizing we weren't alone, Nick looked up at the server. "We're ready to look at the menu now."

We got comfortable in our semi-private area with the heavy wood paneling behind us. Arched windows and dim lights gave it an old Victorian vibe.

Our server handed us our menus. As soon as we placed our order, we had privacy, and Nick put his hand over mine. "I couldn't wait to see you. You really look stunning."

I blushed again.

Moving a strand of hair behind my ear, he looked into my eyes. "Your lips are looking mighty inviting, Miss McAlister."

"Is that why you kiss me every chance you get?"

"What can I say? I need to make up for lost time."

"In that case, I won't be stopping you. Do it whenever you want."

"Sounds like a plan," Nick gave me one of his panty dropping smiles. Then he held out his open palm. "Give me your phone."

Surprised but curious, I took my phone out of my purse and handed it to him.

"What are you going to do?" I asked, slightly suspicious.

For the next minute or so, he typed and swiped. I heard snippets of different ringtones before he handed the phone back to me.

"After everything we went through, it's only fair you have my number saved in your phone. I don't want to be an *unknown caller* anymore."

Embarrassed, I nodded. "I was going to do it tonight."

"Well, I saved you the trouble. All my numbers are on your phone now with different ringtones for each one. That way you have no excuse not to text me back or pick up my calls."

I grinned ear to ear. "I can't make any promises here. My phone is mostly on vibrate if it's even charged. Often, it's not." Wanting to be playful, I stuck my tongue out.

"We need to set some ground rules, Ivy." Nick didn't find my cheekiness funny. "There are some things you can get away with. Making it hard for me to reach you is not one of them. I can't go through the stress of not knowing where you are ever again. That's why I've also set up my number as your emergency contact."

The entire ordeal of him trying to locate me flashed before my eyes.

"Promise me you'll always keep your phone charged and never go anywhere without it."

On the one hand, it felt like he was scolding me. But after making him go through all that, I couldn't do anything but give in.

"I promise. Now, it's my turn." I raised my chin to be more assertive. "It's obvious that I like you…"

"And the feeling is mutual." His smile broadened, reaching all the way to his eyes.

I smiled back. "Now I know. And just so you know, our age has never been a factor for me… until now."

"What are you saying?" His lips pursed immediately. His expression turning grave.

"Let me finish." I didn't want him to close off on me. "I still don't care about that. But you are more experienced and have more power in this relationship than I do."

He wasn't happy with where this was going, but he seemed open to having a discussion. I went on. "I don't feel like an equal in this relationship and it concerns me. Yes, I want to be with you and make this work. But you're really domineering sometimes and it bothers me."

Nick listened intently and took his time before responding. "Ivy, I have many faults and there are many reasons for you not to be with me, but not being an equal can't be one of them. Trust me—you have more power in this relationship than you think. You can set the pace for us and I will follow because I've never wanted anyone the way I want you."

"You mean that?"

"I do, sweetheart. What we have is real. In my entire life, I've never been in a situation I couldn't control; but with you, I'm out of my depth. You feel you have a lot to lose? Believe me, I can lose so much more. But even that won't stop me from dedicating my life to making you happy."

The impact of his words made us both fall silent. Thankfully, our first course arrived, and we now had something to do.

"Do you realize this is our first official date?" I asked, suddenly feeling shy and vulnerable.

"The first of many. And I promise to always be mindful of your feelings. I'll try my best to not give you any reasons to doubt your decision."

That was all I needed to hear.

We got busy eating, talking, and getting to know each other. The conversation flowed like water. He shared stories from his college days. Told me how he and Ryan became best friends, and how they met Jonah and Taber soon after. I learned more about him in the two hours we spent at the restaurant than I had in all my teenage years. It was like we were long-lost friends, which I suppose we were, and now we were getting to connect on an even deeper level.

He listened intently when I told him about my time here in Boston and how close I was to Abby and her family. I had no idea what Abby, Parker, and Nick discussed when I wasn't home, but he only had nice things to say about my friends, which delighted me immensely.

By the time we were done with our dinner, I was a bit tipsy and a whole lot happier. We walked to the parking lot but before he could help me into the car, I wrapped my arms around his neck and pulled him closer. "I have something important to tell you."

He raised an eyebrow. "You do?"

"Mmm." I nodded my head. "I've decided to move back to Manhattan, so I can be closer to you."

Nick's face lit up. He pulled me closer and kissed me until I was blissfully out of breath.

"Thank you. I can't tell you how happy you made me."

"I don't know when I can move, though. Right now, I'm enrolled at Harvard. I have to see if there's any chance of me getting into Columbia at this point. And if I find a way, I still have to go to the admissions office to get started with the transfer process. It's going to take some time."

"I'll take care of it. You don't have to be in Boston for this."

This time, it was my turn to raise eyebrows. "Are you saying that you will get me into Columbia without me actually applying and getting accepted?"

"You're brilliant. You deserve to be a student there. Leave the logistics to me."

"That's what an assassin or a mafia boss would say."

He playfully pinched my cheek. "I will be anything you need me to be, as long as you're by my side."

Like a delicate garland, I encircled my arms around his neck. Sliding my tongue inside his mouth, I kissed him until I got my fill. "Those calls you were getting late at night… were they from Mindy?"

"I was working, sweetheart. Went straight to my office after dropping you at Ryan's. Mindy is history now. You don't need to think about her. Ever." He made me feel at peace.

That reminded me of another discussion. "Is that what Taber and you were discussing at the MoxTo's party?"

He raised an eyebrow. I explained myself. "I was standing with you guys. You two seemed concerned."

"Yes. But I've got enough people working on it already. Nothing you should worry about."

I nodded. His hands slid under my blazer. Changing our discussion, he started caressing my bare back. "Fly with me in the morning."

I loved his smile, his boyish charm. I didn't realize how much I had missed it until now.

"Now you're pushing it, Mr. Branson." I was brimming with desire. His scent was dizzying. "What are you doing to me?"

"I have no idea what you're talking about, Miss Ivy McAlister. I'm as innocent as the clothes you're wearing right now."

His expression made my heart go all gooey. "I haven't packed," I told him.

"Let's go to your apartment and pack."

"Abby is leaving for California in a few weeks. Shouldn't I spend time with her?"

"You can come back and see her before she leaves. And you can always visit her."

"You have a solution for everything, don't you, Mr. Branson?"

"I aim to please, Miss McAlister." Bending down, he gently nipped my cleavage. My breath hitched. "I've been dying to do that since you came to the restaurant," he murmured in my ear, and heat rose in my body.

We drove back to my apartment building. Nick's driver took us to the basement garage, and we got into the elevator. He folded his arms in front of his chest. "Take off your jacket," he ordered.

I let the jacket slide off of me and fall to the ground. After watching endless movies, I knew a thing or two about sexy moves.

His eyes darkened with raw desire and I took that as an invitation to take a step forward.

He radiated heat that my body craved, and yet he didn't move an inch. He just stood there, taking me in.

Looking down at the corset with his heavy-lidded eyes, he said, "Remind me to buy you a dozen of these." Unlocking his arms, he finally closed the distance. His fingers grazed the seam of the corset. Only Nick knew how to arouse me without even touching my skin.

"Turn around."

My breathing grew shallow. I was under his spell once again, turned on by his authoritative voice, following his commands and enjoying every second of it. He pulled the silk tie that held my hair up. Once my locks spilled down my back, he gathered my hair and draped it over my left shoulder, leaving the right side of my neck exposed. Sensitive. Filled with lust.

I didn't know his next move. The anticipation was killing me. I wanted him all over me.

I closed my eyes and felt his warm breath on my bare shoulder, on my neck, and on my ear, provoking all of my senses. I had never been seduced like this before.

"We're here."

It took me a moment to process his words. Confused, I turned around, only to realize that the elevator door had opened. Mr. Irksome stood in the doorway, gloating.

"You're so going to pay for this," I warned him, as I bent down to pick up my jacket.

"Do you accept sexual favors as payment?" he asked, laughing at how frazzled he'd made me.

He put his arm around my shoulders and tried to pull me near him. But wanting to make him pay now, I pushed him away and made a run for the apartment door. Before I could reach it, he pulled me into him and kissed me so passionately that I had to give in.

His face was buried in my hair. I couldn't stop laughing like a teenager. Somehow, I managed to get the keys out of my purse and unlock the door.

Even before I cracked the door open, I felt the visitors.

Too late to turn back now. Hesitantly, I stepped forward, which made Nick knock into me. He steadied himself by holding onto my waist, still laughing.

It took crossing the threshold for him to reach the same conclusion I had reached a moment ago.

Parker was pulling a pizza out of the oven, while Abby, Juan, and—to my horror—Mike, were sitting on the couch and drinking beer.

We had officially stepped into a disaster zone

Chapter 24

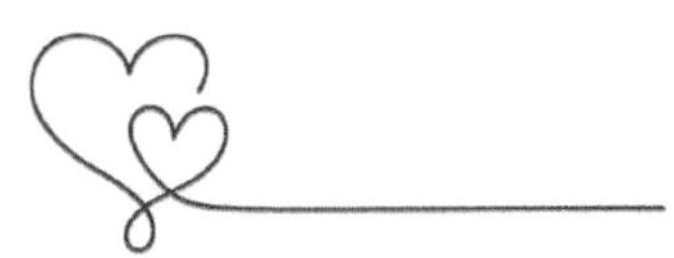

"Oh…hi! I wasn't expecting you to come so soon. We ordered some pizza if you guys want to join," Abby said, and awkwardly rushed over to us.

Our eyes met. She knew what I was thinking. Breaking up with Mike yesterday was one thing, but I didn't want him to think that he meant nothing and that I had moved on this quickly with someone from my past.

"We already ate. Ivy is here to pack her clothes." Nick walked around me and stepped into the apartment.

He shook hands with everybody, including Mike, and introduced himself as Nicholas. Not Nick. Not Branson. Just Nicholas.

"You look so familiar. Have we met before?" Juan asked.

Mike sat down and put the bottle up to his lips. Whatever he felt in this moment, he buried it down deep.

"I don't think so. I'm Ivy's friend." Nick turned toward me. "Do you need help packing?"

"I've got this." My voice was inaudible to my own ear. In a rush, I walked toward my room. When I walked past Mike, our eyes met and I saw it—the hurt and the betrayal.

I did that to him. Will I ever be able to forgive myself for hurting him?

"I'll help you." Abby broke me out of my thoughts.

Once we got to my room, Abby closed the door and sat on my bed. "I'm so sorry. Somehow, I didn't expect to see you so soon. I should've texted you and given you a warning."

Refraining from saying something I would later regret. I took a bag out of my closet and placed it on the bed. My feelings were all over the place. I was mad at Abby for having Mike over. I was embarrassed that he saw me with Nick less than twenty-four hours after we broke up. But most of all, I felt stupid for bringing Nick here.

Thankfully, Abby didn't say anything more and let me pack.

"I'm flying to New York tomorrow morning, with Nick," I told her, when I was ready to talk.

"And how do you feel about it?"

"Happy." I stood still until I couldn't hold it in any longer, and then I ran toward her and hugged her with all my might. "I didn't want to say this since you're so excited, but I'm really going to miss you."

She hugged me back even tighter. "You don't need to tell me how you feel. I know you too well. Trust me, my dear friend— the feeling is mutual."

"I've decided to move back to New York. Permanently." I was already on a roll, so why not give her all the updates at once?

"That's the best decision you could've possibly made." She leaned back against the headboard as I continued packing. "When will I see you again?"

"I'll be back before you leave."

"Fantastic!" she cried, and clapped her hands. "What should I do with your furniture, though? Do you want me to get rid of it?"

"Yes, please. If you don't mind."

"Not at all! I'll take care of it. You go live your life. I mean it, girl. You totally deserve it."

"You're the best." I tossed a few toiletries into the bag. "Now it's my turn to ask questions. Why is Mike here?"

"He called me asking if he could come over to talk. He said that—"

A sharp knock on the door stopped our conversation dead in its tracks.

"Ivy, are you done?" Nick's muffled voice came through the barrier of the door.

"Almost done," I called back. "I'll be out in two!"

I quickly packed the rest of my stuff and hugged Abby again. My life was changing too fast, too soon, but it was already too late to stop it. I had to ride the wave and see where it was going to take me.

"I'll see you soon."

When I opened the door, Nick was standing right outside and waiting for me to come out.

"Were you listening to our conversation?" My tone was tinged with accusation.

He shrugged, not bothering to respond.

An awkward tension had brewed between us by the time we reached the living area. I hugged Juan and Parker and said my goodbyes.

As soon as I approached Mike, who was standing by the balcony looking outside, Nick came up to me from behind, put his hand around my waist in the most possessive way, and pulled me closer.

It was so clear what he was doing. I hated it. Hated him for doing it. Claiming me.

Nick pushed his right hand out to Mike. "It was nice seeing you again."

Mike hesitantly shook his hand, but remained silent. Whatever was keeping him from speaking also kept him from meeting my eyes.

The atmosphere in the room had shifted. Tension was now mixed with confusion and Juan, who had no idea who Nick was until a few minutes ago, was suddenly looking between Mike, Nick, and me.

Nick didn't care. He exchanged pleasantries with Abby and Parker, all the while holding onto me like I was his possession. I didn't have the courage to look at Mike again.

At last, we were out of my apartment and back in the elevator, heading down to where Nick had his car parked. Once the door closed, he took one step toward me and I took two steps back. My shoulder blades met the hard steel wall. It caught him off guard, but he didn't ask why. Probably because he could see that I was fuming with anger. Instead, he turned his back and looked straight ahead.

We reached the car and his driver opened the back door. "Sir."

"I'll drive. See you tomorrow." Without so much as acknowledging him, Nick opened the front passenger door for me.

I slid in without arguing. Hating myself. Hating Nick. Hating this moment.

"You kissed the guy in front of my family. My whole fucking world. You spent an entire evening with him." Nick's venomous voice boomed once we locked ourselves inside his black Range Rover. "Did you really expect me to not let him know that you're mine now?"

"I'm not sure if you realize it, but I'm not a toy."

"No. You're not. But. You. Belong. To. Me." He emphasized his every word. "I made sure there isn't any doubt about that from this point on."

"He's a good man, Nick. No way he deserved that."

"He didn't deserve *you*." The car's engine roared to life. Nick looked straight ahead, shifting into gear.

"Whether he did or didn't is between me and Mike. You can't stick your nose into my business."

"From now on your business *is* my business," he muttered under his breath.

Too frustrated to even look at him, I turned away and faced the window. After all, there was nothing left to discuss.

Doubts started creeping in. Had I made the biggest mistake of my life? How much did I really know about Nick? How long would it be before things got too intense and I ran away again?

The city flashed before me. Boston had been my home for the last eight years and I wouldn't even get a chance to say a proper goodbye.

Tomorrow I'd be back in my hometown, but my excitement was quickly turning into uncertainty. As much as I racked my brain, I couldn't figure out how to make that feeling go away.

I had gotten exactly what I wanted. I was sitting next to the man who had occupied my dreams for years. For so long he had been an unattainable childhood crush, but now that he was with me—into me, obsessed with me, lusting over me—I was no longer sure if I was in love with the real him or with the fictional person I had created in my mind.

Thank you for reading Fate Intertwined! I would really be grateful if you could leave a review on the platforms of your choice. Your reviews are my tips to bring in better books next time.

Much love,

Delia

Read on for a look at the second book in Delia Duke's Intertwined Series:
Fires of Affinity

Was Ivy impulsive in moving to Manhattan for Nick? Will Ivy and Nick stay together? Will Ivy ultimately find what she has been searching for?

These pressing questions set the stage for the second part of the Intertwined Series. In ***Fires of Affinity***, the story of Ivy and Nick's romance unfolds…

As you know, I, Ivy McAlister, came to New York City for a quick visit but ended up moving here to be with the man of my dreams, Nicholas Branson. All in a span of five days!

Was it a hasty decision? Maybe…with Nick behaving erratically and bordering on the bizarre. Sadly, my perfect world with Nick has started to unravel with the realization that everything was not as rosy as I had imagined it to be. As the lines between dreams and reality blurred, I was left to navigate the labyrinth of deception and truth to ascertain if Nick, the billionaire CEO and the most eligible bachelor in Manhattan, and the one I thought was my one true love, is indeed the one that I can truly find happiness with.

Join the mailing list to be the first to preorder Fires of Affinity

Website: https://www.deliadukebooks.com/
Instagram: https://www.instagram.com/deliadukebooks/
Facebook: https://www.facebook.com/profile.php?id=615604 04223427

Acknowledgements

To my husband, Sonny, you have been on my side at every step of the way. Without you, my dream would have only been a dream. Thank you for putting up with me and picking up slack when I am in my zone. (All the time). One day, I will make you read my book as well. It's a hope.

To my daughter, Tyra, for patiently waiting for my attention. There are times you have survived on Z-bars because Mumma was busy writing. You took everything in your stride. I hope you learn the power of grit. Finish what you start and never look back.

To Ieva, Janeen O'Kerry, and the entire team, without your hard work and support, this book wouldn't have seen the day of light.

To my friends and beta readers, Piya, Amy, Sarada, Swas, Becca, and Miranda, without your feedback, this book wouldn't have been as complete.

And the last, but not the least, my readers. Thank you for coming along on this journey with me. For trusting me to deliver you something that you enjoyed. I look forward to our long relationship here on.

About the author

A new and upcoming author, Delia writes contemporary romance with a deliciously stubborn alpha male, strong female, and plenty of streams and angst.

A travel enthusiast and a foodie at heart, she loves incorporating her life experiences into her stories and will never say no to girls' night out.

An analyst by day and a writer by night, if she is not working, you will find her traveling the world with her family or eating out with her friends.

To know more about Delia please visit her website @ https://www.deliadukebooks.com/